Blau

THE SPIDER SAPPHIRE MYSTERY

THRILLING, dangerous adventures confront Nancy Drew while on a safari in East Africa with a group of American college students. Excitement runs high as the teen-age detective delves into the theft of a fabulous sapphire formed by nature millions of years ago.

The mystery starts in Nancy's home town. Her lawyer father's client, Floyd Ramsey, who fashions beautiful and unusual synthetic gems, is accused of stealing the magnificent spider sapphire and exhibiting it as his own creation. Mr. Ramsey's enemies blackmail him and by their vicious acts try to deter Nancy from going on the safari.

How the daring young sleuth uncovers a nefarious scheme and also solves the strange disappearance of an injured jungle guide will keep the reader breathless with suspense from first page to last.

Nancy's struggles to free herself were in vain

NANCY DREW MYSTERY STORIES

The Spider Sapphire Mystery

BY CAROLYN KEENE

PUBLISHERS   *Grosset & Dunlap*   NEW YORK

Contents

The
Spider Sapphire
Mystery

CHAPTER I

Stolen Gem

NANCY Drew drove her convertible into the public parking lot and chose a space facing the far fence. There were few cars at this hour, since the early-morning shoppers had left.

As the attractive, titian-haired girl turned off the motor and took the key from the ignition lock, a car pulled in on each side of her. In an instant Nancy realized that they were parked so close she could not open either of her doors. The two drivers immediately jumped out and hurried away.

Nancy called to them. "Wait a minute! You've parked so I can't get out!"

The men paid no attention. She honked her horn loudly, but they did not turn their heads.

"How inconsiderate!" Nancy thought angrily. "And with the parking lot almost empty."

She caught a glimpse of the two men. They were dark-complexioned and she guessed they

1

were from India. One looked to be about twenty years old, the other forty.

"Well," Nancy said to herself, "I'll just have to back out of here and find another place."

She put the key into the ignition lock and started the motor. At that instant a car came whizzing into the parking lot, turned sideways abruptly, and stopped directly behind her.

Nancy leaned out the window and called, "I want to get out of here!"

She could not see the driver, but she was sure he had heard her. Instead of moving his car, he jumped out and sped across the parking lot to the street. He was a large, well-built, dark-skinned man. She could not see his face.

With a sigh Nancy decided she would have to put down the top of her convertible and crawl over one of the cars. Then she remembered that before leaving home she had tried the mechanism and it had failed to work.

"I must stop at the garage on my way home," she decided.

Suddenly Nancy realized she was a prisoner. It also occurred to her that the whole episode had been planned by the three men.

"But why?" she asked herself.

Nancy sat lost in thought for a full minute. Her father, Carson Drew, a prominent lawyer, had recently taken an interesting case. There was a unique mystery attached to it. Was she being ha-

Nancy realized she was a prisoner

rassed to make her father give up the case? Nancy wondered. She had become well known as an amateur sleuth. Perhaps the people connected with the mystery had found this out and intended to keep her from helping her father.

"Whatever the motive, I'm stuck here right now," she told herself. "How am I to get out of this car?"

Nancy knew she would need help. She pressed the horn and let it blow continuously. Sooner or later someone would come to see about stopping the noise.

The person who arrived was a young policeman. Nancy did not know him, although she was acquainted with many of the men on the River Heights force. She had often worked directly with Chief McGinnis.

"What's going on here?" the officer asked cheerfully. "Somebody playing a joke on you?"

"I think not," Nancy replied. Quickly she told what had happened, and added, "I believe this was deliberate."

"My name is Orton," the policeman said. "I'll get you out of here as fast as I can."

He tried the doors of all three cars. Every one of them was locked.

Orton pulled a book from his pocket and began comparing numbers in it with the license plates on the three cars. Finally he said, "Just what I suspected. Each of these cars is listed as stolen."

He said he would make a report to headquarters at once and a locksmith would be sent to open the doors. After he had gone Nancy fumed over the trick that had been played on her. In the future she must be more careful about traps.

About ten minutes later Orton returned with the locksmith and another policeman. While various keys were being tried, Orton asked Nancy for a description of the three men who had driven into the parking lot.

"I'm afraid it will be pretty sketchy," she replied, but told him what little she knew.

"They could be foreigners, especially the Indians," the officer stated. "Chief McGinnis will probably get in touch with the immigration authorities."

The three cars were finally moved and Nancy, relieved, stepped to the pavement.

"Thanks a million," she said to the three men. "I hope you catch those car thieves."

Nancy was convinced that the strangers were more than mere car thieves. She would talk the matter over later with her father.

She continued on to her destination, the River Heights Museum. Her father had told her about an amazing gem on display there. It was a huge sapphire with a spider embedded in it.

"To think that this rare piece of work is only synthetic," Nancy murmured. "Dad said it was made by Mr. Floyd Ramsey, who fashions beautiful and unusual synthetic jewelry, right here in River Heights."

The mystery which her father had hinted at concerned Mr. Ramsey and a wealthy Indian in Africa who owned a genuine sapphire with a spider embedded in it.

"I can't wait to hear the rest of the story," Nancy thought as she walked along Maple Avenue toward the museum.

She heard someone across the street whistle. Thinking it might be her friend Ned Nickerson, Nancy turned to look. At that instant someone banged into her from the rear, snatched her purse, and tried to knock her down. As Nancy teetered to regain her balance, the thief dashed down the street.

"He's the younger of the two Indians who penned me in!" she thought. Nancy started running after him, crying out, "Stop thief!"

A man, coming from the opposite direction, heard her. Seeing the purse clutched under one arm of the fleeing figure, he stopped the Indian and grabbed the bag, but it dropped to the pavement. He struggled to hold onto the thief, but with a neat judo shoulder throw, the purse snatcher tossed the man onto the sidewalk. Then the Indian fled around the corner.

Horrified onlookers were helping the man to his feet as Nancy ran up to him. "I'm dreadfully sorry," she said. "Are you hurt?"

The man smiled. "Only my pride." He picked up the handbag and handed it to Nancy.

A patrolman rushed to the scene and asked for the story. When Nancy stated that this was the second time within an hour that she had been annoyed by the same man, the officer took notes and he said he would telephone the information to headquarters at once. By this time the crowd had melted away.

The stranger who had come to her assistance refused to give his name. Smiling, he said, "I don't want any publicity. It was my privilege to help a young lady."

With a wave of his hand he strode off. As Nancy walked on, she reflected about people of good and bad intent who so often crossed her path.

Presently Nancy smiled to herself. "Hannah always says that things come in threes. I wonder what's in store for me now."

Hannah Gruen, the Drews' housekeeper, had lived with Nancy and her father since the death of Mrs. Drew when Nancy was three years old. The warm-hearted woman was like a mother to Nancy and worried constantly about the strange situations which the young sleuth faced when solving mysteries.

"Poor Hannah!" Nancy thought. "She'll be so upset when I tell her what happened this morning."

By now Nancy had reached the museum. The

curator, Mr. Sand, was standing in the entrance hall.

"Good morning, Nancy," he said. "Have you come to see Mr. Ramsey's gem?"

"Yes, I have," Nancy replied. "I understand it's exquisite."

The curator nodded. "I defy anyone to tell the gem from an original. You'll find it in the room to the right of the one where the prehistoric animals are."

Nancy hurried through the big room and turned into the smaller one. A glass case stood in the center. On a mound of white velvet lay the unique gem.

Before Nancy had a chance to examine it carefully through the glass, a homemade printed sign tacked to one corner of the case caught her attention. She read it and frowned, puzzled. The sign said:

THIS GEM WAS STOLEN

CHAPTER II

Missing Student

THE curator had followed Nancy to the spider sapphire case.

"Well, what do you think of—" Mr. Sand began. He stopped speaking abruptly as Nancy pointed to the sign saying the gem had been stolen.

The man's face turned red with anger. "That is not true!" he cried. "Someone put the sign there—someone who is trying to cause trouble!"

He called to a guard standing near the door and quizzed him about recent visitors. "Everybody looked all right to me," the guard answered. He smiled. "Maybe some teen-ager put that up there for a joke."

"Maybe," the curator agreed, calming down.

Nancy was inclined to disagree, but did not voice this opinion to the others. She asked the guard to describe all the men who had been in the museum recently.

Her pulse quickened when he said, "One of the visitors looked to me like a native of India. He kept walking around and around the case and seemed mighty interested in the gem."

This was all the proof Nancy needed. The Indian visitor fitted the description of the older of the two men who had imprisoned her in the car.

After the guard had gone back to the door, she said to Mr. Sand, "I don't trust that Indian. If he ever returns, watch him carefully."

The curator smiled. "You're mixed up again in some mystery and this time it involves an Indian?" he asked.

Nancy did not reply. She merely gave the man a wink.

The young detective rarely discussed her cases with anyone except her father, closest friends, or police and detectives. Mr. Drew had given her this advice on her first case, *The Secret of the Old Clock,* and Nancy had followed his wise counsel in solving all her other cases, including the most recent one, *The Clue in the Crossword Cipher.*

Nancy now gave her full attention to the magnificent, almost round, inch-long gem in the case with the spider embedded in it. The sapphire, a shade darker than pale blue, sparkled brilliantly. The gem was transparent except where the spider lay. A card in the display case stated that Mr.

Floyd Ramsey had produced this sapphire synthetically.

"The gem is absolutely beautiful," she said to Mr. Sand. "What gave Mr. Ramsey the idea of embedding a spider in the sapphire?"

"He saw a picture of a similar gem—a real one —and decided to experiment to see if he could imitate it."

After a pause Mr. Sand remarked, "You know, spiders are one of the oldest living creatures on earth. They appeared at least three hundred million years ago."

"Really?" Nancy asked, amazed.

The curator said that the study of spiders was intriguing. "The whole earth is covered with them. They're man's best friend. If spiders weren't around, we'd be overrun and eaten up with insects."

Amused by Nancy's frown, Mr. Sand went on, "I read recently that a man in England made a study of spiders to determine how many there were in a certain area. A census of one acre was two and a quarter million spiders!"

Nancy gasped. Then she laughed. "Mr. Sand, you make me feel positively crawly."

The curator's eyes twinkled. "Do you know how old the world's sapphires are—I mean the kind that Mother Nature fashioned?"

Nancy shook her head. "How old?"

"So far as is known they first appeared in the

Carboniferous Era. That's roughly two hundred and fifty million years ago."

"So spiders and sapphires are much older than man," Nancy observed. "I believe human beings first appeared on the earth ten million years ago."

"That's right."

Mr. Sand was summoned to the telephone and Nancy spent a few more minutes admiring the spider sapphire.

"I must go to Dad's office and ask him all about the spider sapphire mystery," she told herself, and left the museum.

She found tall, athletic Mr. Drew dictating a letter to one of his secretaries, Miss Hanson. Nancy offered to wait in the reception room, but he insisted that both she and Miss Hanson remain.

"You never come here unless you have something important on your mind," he teased Nancy. "What is it this time?"

His daughter told about the "stolen" sign tacked onto the spider sapphire case.

"It may involve the ancient spider sapphire owned by the Indian, Shastri Tagore," the lawyer said. "His agents are in this country. They revealed the theft of his gem. These agents, who are Indians, live in Mombasa, East Africa, where Mr. Tagore has a home. They had heard about the gem Mr. Ramsey claimed he made. The men don't believe his story and insist that the gem is Mr. Tagore's stolen property."

"But you believe Mr. Ramscy, don't you?" Nancy asked.

"Of course I do. I have known Floyd for a long time. There's not a more honest man in the world."

Nancy had not intended to tell her father about the purse-snatching incident, but he surprised her by saying, "I hear a man grabbed your handbag and almost knocked you down."

Mr. Drew added that someone who had seen the incident had called him and related the story.

"I hope the person also told you about the nice man who retrieved my bag. And here's a story I'm sure you haven't heard."

Nancy told him of her experience in the parking lot and her suspicion that the man who had grabbed her handbag was one of the drivers. It was the lawyer's turn to look amazed, and Miss Hanson gasped.

"I'm sure the whole thing is bound up with the spider sapphire mystery," Nancy told her father.

"Then I'm glad you're going away so soon," Mr. Drew said. "In the meantime I insist that you have someone with you whenever you leave the house."

Miss Hanson spoke up. "Oh, you're going away, Nancy?"

"Yes, on an African safari. Isn't it marvelous?"

"Will you be with a group?" the secretary inquired.

Nancy nodded. "You know that my friend Ned Nickerson attends Emerson College. The safari has been organized by some of the professors. Boys who are majoring in botany, zoology, and geology are making the trip. They're being allowed to ask friends to go at the students' rate. Bess and George and I have signed up. Burt and Dave, their dates, will be along, too."

"It sounds thrilling," Miss Hanson remarked.

Nancy said that the leaders of the Emerson safari were Professor and Mrs. Wilmer Stanley. "He's always called Prof and she's affectionately known as Aunt Millie to the boys."

"It certainly sounds like fun," Miss Hanson remarked as she picked up the telephone which had started to ring.

Mr. Drew and Nancy stopped speaking. Miss Hanson said, "Mr. Drew's office. . . . She's here. Do you wish to speak to her?" Then the secretary became silent. Presently her brow furrowed. Finally she said, "Thank you. I'll tell her."

Miss Hanson put down the phone and looked directly at Nancy. "The call was from Professor Stanley. He said he was in a hurry and wouldn't take time to speak to you. I'm terribly sorry to give you his message, Nancy. Ned Nickerson can't go on the safari after all."

Nancy's heart sank. What had happened? She forced herself to say, "That is bad news." She had talked to Ned only two days before and he was extremely eager to go on the safari. He had said, "Nothing in this world will keep me from going."

Mr. Drew declared that it was strange Ned had not telephoned Nancy direct. Why should he have asked Professor Stanley to make the call?

Nancy's suspicions were aroused at once. She asked Miss Hanson to put in a call to the college and ask for Professor Stanley. It took some time to locate him, but finally the secretary reached the professor at his home.

"Miss Drew wishes to speak to you," Miss Hanson told him.

"Hello, Nancy," he said genially. "How are you? All ready for the trip?"

"Yes, I'm ready. But what's all this about Ned not going?"

"What do you mean?" the professor asked.

"Didn't you phone my father's office during the past few minutes?"

"Why no."

When she told what had occurred, Professor Stanley said of course Ned was going. Someone was just playing a prank.

Nancy doubted this but made no comment. She said she would be seeing the professor soon and hung up. Next, Nancy asked Miss Hanson to call Ned at the Omega Chi Epsilon Fraternity House at Emerson.

When the connection was made, Nancy learned that Ned was not there, so she asked for Burt Eddleton.

When he came on the wire, she told him what had happened. Burt was amazed at the story and also disturbed.

"Ned left the dorm yesterday afternoon. Later he phoned and gave someone a message that he was going home. I don't like this at all," Burt added.

"I'll call the Nickersons right away and see if he's there," Nancy said.

She spoke to Mrs. Nickerson, who said that her son had not come home and she had not heard from him. Because Nancy did not want to alarm his parents unnecessarily, she did not express the fear which was forming in her mind. Ned might have met with foul play!

CHAPTER III

The 4182 Code

ALTHOUGH Mrs. Nickerson tried to remain calm, Nancy could tell that she was disturbed by the news. "It's unlike Ned not to be in touch with his father and me and his friends."

"I'll ask Bess and George to go with me to Emerson tomorrow morning and help search—if that's necessary," Nancy told her.

"I'm glad to know that," Ned's father said on their extension phone. "If you hear from him, please ask him to phone us."

Nancy promised to do so, then hung up and turned to her father. "What do you think I should do now?" she inquired. "I have a strong hunch something is wrong."

"Why don't you telephone Burt and Dave? Ask them to make a thorough search of the campus to see if they can locate Ned."

Miss Hanson was already reaching for the telephone and again dialed the number of the Omega Chi Epsilon house. She asked for Burt Eddleton and Dave Evans. Both came on the wire and Nancy told them that Ned had not come home.

"I'm afraid he may have met with foul play," she said. "Would you make a thorough search of the campus and let me know what you find out?"

Neither of the boys answered at once and she could hear them whispering in the background. Finally Dave said, "That's kind of a large order, Nancy. Perhaps we should get all our fraternity brothers to help in the search. And maybe we should report this to the police."

Burt spoke up. "Personally I feel that Ned went off of his own accord to study. He'd be mighty embarrassed having a whole bunch of us burst in on him. You know we're all cramming for exams. We have a tough one coming up tomorrow morning."

There was another long pause, during which a plan was formulating in Nancy's mind. At last she said, "Would it help if Bess and George and I come up to help search—that is, if you don't find any trace of Ned this afternoon?"

Burt said this was exactly what the boys had hoped she might suggest. "We'll get busy at once and let you know at suppertime what we find out."

Nancy's next call was to Bess, who was astounded at the news. She agreed at once to go to

Emerson. Her cousin, George Fayne, an athletic-looking girl, was eager to help.

"Great," said Nancy. "I'll let you know as soon as I hear from Dave and Burt."

The afternoon hours dragged by. Nancy took her convertible to be repaired so the top would raise and lower again. The mechanic said it had been tampered with and Nancy was sure the sabotage had been committed in the Drews' garage. "And by those men who imprisoned me in the parking lot!"

In her alarm over Ned, Nancy had forgotten about the African safari and the spider sapphire mystery. The whole thing came back to her as she packed a few clothes into a suitcase and talked to Hannah Gruen. The housekeeper was dismayed by the strange turn of events.

"No doubt about it," she said. "There are villains in this picture somewhere. The extent to which some people will go to gain dishonest ends is frightening. Please, Nancy, promise me that you will be very careful."

Nancy smiled and hugged the housekeeper, for whom she had a deep affection. "I promise."

At seven o'clock the telephone rang and Nancy ran to answer it. Burt was calling. There was a note of deep concern in his voice. Twenty-five boys had taken part in a thorough search of the campus. They had not found Ned.

"Nancy, do you think he has been kidnapped?" Burt asked.

She closed her eyes as if to shut out the dreadful thought and said, "It looks so. I'll get in touch with the Nickersons immediately."

With a heavy heart Nancy dialed the number of the Nickerson home. This time Ned's father answered. Though he tried to keep his voice steady, it was evident he was apprehensive over his son's safety when he heard the upsetting news.

"Bess and George and I are driving up to Emerson early tomorrow morning," Nancy told him. "Will you be going too?"

After talking with his wife, Mr. Nickerson said he thought not. They had concluded that if Ned had been kidnapped, a demand for ransom would come to the house. They wanted to be home to receive any messages.

"And we figure it's too soon to notify the police—at least before we get a ransom note."

Nancy said the three girls would make an extensive search of the area around Emerson. "Burt and Dave will join us in the hunt as soon as their exams are over. I'll let you know what we learn," she promised.

"And I'll call your father if we receive a ransom note," Mr. Nickerson said.

No word came during the night and everyone in the Drew household arose early. Nancy did not feel like eating breakfast but her father and Hannah Gruen insisted.

"It's a long drive to Emerson and you'll need all your strength," the housekeeper stated.

Just before six o'clock Nancy stopped her convertible in front of Bess Marvin's home. At once the front door opened and the pretty, blond-haired girl came out to the car, carrying a rather large suitcase.

"Hello, Nancy. Please forgive the big bag. No telling how long this mystery may last. Oh, isn't it terrible? I think this is the worst mission you've ever asked me to go on with you."

"I'm afraid it is." Nancy was grim.

There was little conversation for the next few blocks as they rode to George Fayne's house. The slender, dark-haired girl ran down the steps, swinging a small overnight bag which she tossed into the back of the convertible, then hopped in.

Once on the highway, Nancy kept to the speed limit and the miles flew past quickly. By noon the three girls had reached Emerson and checked in at the Longview Motel.

"Let's start work right away," Nancy urged, as soon as they had eaten lunch. "I think we should go to the railroad and the bus station to ask if anyone saw Ned go out of town day before yesterday."

When nothing was learned from these sources,

the girls went to two rent-a-car agencies and made inquiries. No one answering Ned's description had rented a car the day he disappeared.

"I'm tired," said Bess. "Let's go back to the motel and rest, then start out again."

When the girls reached the Longview, Nancy said she would call the Nickersons. "I hate to report failure, but they may have some word by this time."

Ned's parents had heard nothing. Mr. Nickerson said that if they did not hear from Ned by nighttime, they would notify the police. They were almost certain that Ned had been kidnapped. But by whom and why?

"It begins to look as if the kidnappers were not after money," Mr. Nickerson stated. "Nancy, have you any theories about the reason?"

"Yes, I have," she answered. It may be a farfetched idea, but there's a possibility that a mystery I might work on in Africa is the answer. The kidnappers may feel that by keeping Ned from going, I would stay home." In a moment she added, "And I would, too."

Presently Nancy said good-by. As she came from the phone booth, Burt and Dave walked into the motel lobby. "Any luck?" they asked.

Nancy shook her head. "If we only had one little tiny clue—"

"We have!" the two boys cried together.

Burt said that a short while ago, when they

returned to the fraternity house after the exam, they had received a phone call. The caller's voice was quick and muffled, but they were sure he had been Ned Nickerson.

"What did he say?" Nancy asked as Bess and George hurried up to the trio.

"The message sounded like 'Swahili Joe pair 4182.' "

"What does that mean?" Bess spoke up. "If Ned could talk to you, why didn't he tell you something you could understand?"

Nancy said that perhaps Ned was afraid the place where he was being held prisoner was bugged and he did not dare give the location except through this code.

"It's not going to be an easy one to crack," Dave remarked. "Who is Swahili Joe?"

"My guess," said George, "is he's the kidnapper."

Burt offered to telephone the local police and ask if they had ever heard of such a person. He soon returned to say that no one at headquarters had ever heard of a Swahili Joe.

"They thought he might be a restaurant owner or barber, but there's no record of anyone by that name."

"It's probably a nickname," Dave suggested.

The five young people talked at great length about the strange name and finally Nancy said she would get in touch with her father. "I'll ask him to contact the Immigration Department and find out if Swahili Joe is an African who entered the United States from some country where Swahili's spoken."

As she left to make the call, George came up with another theory. The numerals 4182 might be part of a phone number. "It will take us forever to go through the book but let's try."

When Nancy rejoined them she too started to look. The task seemed endless.

Bess sighed. "We're getting no place fast," she mumbled. "Nancy, what did your father say?"

"He's going to get in touch with the FBI as well as the immigration authorities. He said he'd call me back, so I guess we'll have to stay here for a while."

It was three o'clock when the call came. Mr. Drew told Nancy that no person nicknamed Swahili Joe was known to have entered the United States.

Nancy asked her father if there had been any more news about the case of the spider sapphire. When he answered No, she said:

"Dad, do you think there could be a fraud in connection with this whole thing?"

CHAPTER IV

New Interpretation

THERE was silence on the wire for several seconds before Mr. Drew spoke. Do you mean that perhaps the real spider sapphire wasn't stolen?" he asked his daughter.

Nancy said that it might be an insurance fraud. The owner of the gem, working either alone or with some other men, might have reported to the insurance company that the jewel had been stolen.

"Then he'd collect a large amount of money for it," Nancy stated.

Later on the sapphire would be sold secretly to some unscrupulous person. The buyer might break up the huge gem into smaller stones and sell them.

"Your hunch is a very good one, Nancy," the lawyer answered. "At this stage no one really knows. Suppose I tell you the whole story."

"Please do," Nancy requested.

Mr. Drew said that two men had come to call on Mr. Ramsey.

"They said they were emissaries of the owner of the spider sapphire, Mr. Tagore. Their names are Jahan and Dhan. They were born in India but live in Mombasa, Africa.

"Mr. Ramsey was amazed and angry when the two men accused him of stealing the owner's gem and exhibiting it as a synthetic sapphire."

"The nerve of them!" Nancy burst out. "What did Mr. Ramsey do?"

"He called in several of his company employees, who also vigorously denied the accusation, saying that Mr. Ramsey was a genius and indeed had fashioned the synthetic spider sapphire himself."

"Then what happened?" Nancy asked.

Mr. Drew told her that at this point Jahan and Dhan had apologized for being so hasty, but came up with a new theory. "They now accused Mr. Ramsey of having borrowed the original from the thief and used it as a model for his own gem."

"That's even worse!" Nancy exclaimed.

Her father agreed. "Of course Mr. Ramsey denied their claim, but Mr. Dhan with a smooth sort of smile said, 'Mr. Ramsey, if you will give us back the original gem, or the money it is worth, we promise not to say anything to the authorities. Certainly you want to avoid unpleasant publicity.' "

"That sounds serious," Nancy remarked. "What happened then?"

"By that time Mr. Ramsey had become very suspicious. He said he would have to think over the whole matter and asked the men to return in a few days.

"Mr. Ramsey came to me at once with the entire story. I decided to get in touch with the owner of the real spider sapphire, but was told he was away on vacation and his secretary, a man named Rhim Rao, also an Indian, was taking care of his affairs."

"Did he confirm Jahan and Dhan's story?" Nancy queried.

"Yes, he did." While he, too, had been polite, Rhim Rao insisted that Mr. Tagore's spider sapphire had been stolen and suspicion most certainly pointed to Mr. Ramsey. "I could not convince him that the synthetic gem had been made right here in River Heights," the lawyer added.

Mr. Drew said that he had been in Mr. Ramsey's office when Jahan and Dhan had returned. He, as attorney for Mr. Ramsey, and to test the Indians' honesty, had insisted upon some kind of proof from the two foreigners before any discussion could take place. "They promised to bring some, but of course they never did. I engaged a detective to trail them, but unfortunately they managed to slip away."

Nancy asked her father if he thought this meant Jahan and Dhan had left the country.

"Possibly, but not under their own names—or at least the names of Jahan and Dhan. I checked with the immigration authorities."

Nancy continued to think about the strange story as she said good-by to Mr. Drew and returned to her friends in the lounge of the Longview Motel. They were so busy discussing how to go about finding Ned Nickerson that Nancy decided not to tell them her father's story now. Each one in the group made several wild guesses as to what the strange message from Ned could mean.

Suddenly Burt spoke up excitedly. "Hey, I just thought of something. Maybe we're figuring on the wrong pair. Ned could have meant *p-a-r-e*."

"You could be right," Dave replied, "but what's he going to cut off? It leaves us just as confused as ever."

"He could also have meant *p-e-a-r*," George stated.

"True," said Bess. "But what would he have meant by that?"

George could not resist the temptation to tease her cousin. "You love to eat. The answer should be easy for you."

Bess was used to George's gibes and invariably they piqued Bess into coming up with an answer.

This time was no exception. With a toss of her head, she said, "How about a pear orchard?"

"Brilliant idea," Dave praised her. "But how are we going to locate the right pear orchard?"

"I might have an answer to that," Nancy spoke up.

"Then out with it," Burt urged. "The sooner we find Ned the better."

Nancy asked, "Wasn't Ned doing some map making in connection with one of his courses?"

"Yes, he was," Dave replied. "How does that apply here?"

Nancy smiled. "In map making you use latitude and longitude."

"Right," Burt agreed. "But what's the connection?"

Nancy's answer amazed the others. "Those numbers 4182. They might mean latitude and longitude."

"Boy, that's a brilliant idea!" Dave burst out.

"It sure is," George spoke up. "Let's find a map of this area."

The manager of the motel supplied one. The young people spread it out on a table in the lobby. Nancy ran her finger along the longitude line while George ran hers up the one for latitude. Their fingers met at a point several miles from Emerson.

"That's it!" Burt cried. "Let's go!"

The five young sleuths set off in Nancy's convertible. There were main highways only part of the distance. Then it became necessary to take bumpy, country roads. The last part of the journey was a long, very narrow stretch with a deep ravine on their side.

"I hope we don't meet anybody," Bess said nervously. "Whatever would we do?"

The words were hardly out of her mouth when they heard the roar of a motor around the bend just ahead. Nancy, who was driving, began to blow the convertible's horn. In a moment a truck pulled up in front of her and stopped.

The driver proved to be a farmer. Nancy got out and walked up to him.

"This is unfortunate," she said. "What are we going to do?"

The farmer scowled. "What are *we* going to do? You mean what are *you* going to do?"

Nancy stared at the unpleasant man. "I'm not familiar with this road. You must be. Is there a turnoff anywhere?"

"No," he answered. "I'll tell you what you're going to do. Get in that car of yours and back up."

By this time Burt and Dave had jumped out of the convertible.

"We're on the ravine side," Burt spoke up. "Couldn't you just pull your truck off the road a little so we can pass?"

"And maybe break a wheel or overturn?" the farmer cried out. "I should say not. Besides, I'm in a hurry. I got to get to market."

"You're asking us to back up for a whole mile," Dave protested.

"That's exactly what I want you to do. And you'd better be quick about it!" the man shouted.

Nancy was dismayed. While it was not impossible for her to back up a mile, it seemed unnecessary. She was sure that if the farmer would pull off the road a little, he would neither break a wheel nor upset. He was being very unreasonable.

"Oh, this is dreadful!" Bess wailed.

The argument ceased when they heard another car coming along the road in back of Nancy's convertible. The newcomer was a State Police officer. Quickly scanning the scene, he stepped up to the group and asked, "What's the trouble here?"

"These kids won't back up to let me pass!" the farmer growled.

Nancy was about to speak up when the officer said to the farmer, "I think it would be much simpler if you pull over and let these people pass."

The farmer, muttering under his breath, got back into his truck and pulled off the road. After thanking the policeman, the others returned to their car and continued their journey, with the officer following. At a crossroad the policeman turned off and waved to the young people.

"How much farther is it?" George asked.

Burt consulted the map. "Four-one-eight-two should be right ahead."

When Nancy pulled around a turn in the road past a little hill, Bess exclaimed, "A pear orchard!"

The trees were filled with white blossoms. On the other side of the road, a few feet below the edge, a brook gurgled along.

Everyone was tense. Which way should they go to search for Ned? Along the brook or through the pear orchard?

Before anyone had a chance to get out of the car, a sedan suddenly roared up behind them. Two revolvers poked from the windows and shots were fired at the tires of Nancy's convertible. The next moment four masked men leaped from the sedan and surrounded her car.

One of the men ordered in a gruff voice, "Get out and follow us!"

CHAPTER V

Suspicious Initials

KNOWING that it would be foolhardy to resist the armed men, Nancy and her friends started walking down the road. Two of the holdup men were in front, the two with the revolvers in the rear. Burt and Dave exchanged glances, then looked at the girls.

All the young people understood the message: If there was any opportunity for them to attack their captors, they were to do it at a signal from Burt.

In a few moments the men with the revolvers put the weapons into their pockets and seemed to relax. Apparently they did not expect any trouble from their prisoners.

Suddenly Burt's hand went up in the air. Quick as a flash, he tackled the largest of the men. Dave took a tall man, while George in a surprise move toward one of the two shorter men used a judo twist on him. The mask fell from his face.

Nancy and Bess together had pinned the arms of the fourth man behind him. As they grabbed the mask from his face, Nancy gasped.

He was one of the men who had hemmed in her car! Out of the corner of her eye, she saw that the man George had swung to the ground was the other Indian!

In lightning moves the two suspects pulled away from the girls and ran as fast as they could through the pear orchard.

"Let's chase them!" George urged.

"Better not," Burt mumbled between punches. "Don't forget—they're armed."

"Not now they aren't!" Bess exclaimed.

She pointed to the ground where two revolvers had fallen from the men's pockets. Nancy and George picked up the weapons and flung them down into the brook.

Although the boys had won the first round, they were having a struggle to keep from being beaten in the fight. At once George went to help Burt subdue his man. Then she ripped off his mask. He was about thirty years old, fair-skinned, and had blond hair.

Nancy and Bess helped Dave. His assailant proved to be white also. "Who are you?" Nancy asked.

"There was no answer. She put the same question to the other attacker, but he too remained silent.

"Nancy, have you any rope in your car?" Burt asked.

She nodded. "There's some in the trunk."

"Will you please get it. I think we should tie these men up until we can get the police."

The hands of the attackers were tied behind their backs. Then the men's ankles were firmly bound together with rope.

Burt asked Nancy to drive to the nearest road-side phone and summon the police. She drove several miles along the country road but there was no place to make a telephone call. Finally she came to a farmhouse and asked the woman there if she might use the telephone.

"Yes. Come right in."

Upon hearing Nancy's report to the police, the woman was full of questions. Nancy answered as much as she thought advisable, then excused herself and hurried back to the group.

George told her, "We tried to catch these men off guard and asked them who Swahili Joe is. But they only looked blank. I guess they don't know him."

A few minutes later two State Police cars arrived with four officers. One of them, who said his name was Riggi, recognized the two prisoners as town thugs from nearby Landsdowne.

Nancy took Officer Riggi aside and told him

about the two Indians who had escaped. "They may lead us to a friend of ours who was kidnapped," she added.

Riggi was amazed and said he and Officer White would join Nancy's group in their search. The other two officers would take the prisoners to Landsdowne.

The car which they had used belonged to one of the thugs. Riggi ordered that the gas be drained from it, the air let out of the tires, and the key taken so that if the two Indians came back to use it, they would find this impossible.

"What about your car?" Officer Riggi asked Nancy. "The men might steal it."

"I'll fix that," Nancy replied. "There's a secret switch under the dash that locks the wheels." She turned it, then locked all the doors.

"And now let's go," said Riggi.

He and Officer White looked for footprints of the two escapees. Presently they picked them up and the group quickly went through the pear orchard. At the far end of it stood a cabin which appeared to be abandoned. The police tried the doors and windows. All were locked.

At the top of his voice, Riggi ordered anyone inside to come out at once. No one appeared and there was utter silence.

"I guess we'll have to force open a window," Officer White said. He did this and reported that there was no one inside the building.

Meanwhile, Nancy hurried down the stepping stones which led from the rear door of the cabin. At the end of the path, Nancy found what she suspected might be there—four sets of footprints in the dirt beyond.

"Come here, everybody!" she called.

The others hurried to where she was pointing and Officer Riggi said, "Hm! You're quite a detective."

Nancy smiled her thanks. "If my friend Ned Nickerson was being held here, I believe those two Indians took him away. Let's hurry!"

The prints were easy to follow. Everyone was excited. Were they near the end of the search? Dave had just expressed this thought when the footprints ended abruptly at a wide brook.

"Oh dear!" Bess exclaimed. "Now what do we do?"

"I believe," said Nancy, "that if it was Ned who was here, he would have tried in some way to leave a sign to tell us which direction to take."

"But how could he if he was a prisoner?" George asked.

Nancy did not answer. She was examining the ground and the trees in the area. Suddenly she cried out, "Here's a clue on the trunk of this tree."

Crudely marked but plain enough were the initials SJ. Underneath was an arrow pointing to the left.

"Those aren't Ned's initials," said Dave. "Whose are they?"

The three girls chorused, "Swahili Joe's."

Dave shook his head in bewilderment. "I'm more confused than ever. If Ned did this, why would he put Swahili Joe's initials here instead of his own? And how would he know which way they would head?"

"You're really asking me a hard one," said Nancy. "All I can do is guess. When the three men got here, the two Indians tied Ned to this tree while they refreshed themselves in the brook and talked over their plans. Ned felt that it would not be safe to scratch his own initials, but we'd recognize SJ if we were able to follow his clues."

The two police officers looked at her admiringly. "You know, Miss Drew," said Riggi, "you ought to be a secret agent."

"I'd love that," Nancy said quickly.

"But we wouldn't," Bess spoke up. "You get into enough trouble just being a girl detective."

The group wasted no more time. Following Nancy's hunch, they turned in the direction of the arrow and hurried along the brook. The kidnappers they were trying to overtake had apparently walked in the water with Ned because there were no more footprints. The searchers had covered nearly two miles and still had found nothing to indicate where Ned might be now.

Bess said her feet hurt. She had not worn suit-

"Here's a clue!" Nancy cried out

able shoes for tramping in the woods and had turned her ankle several times.

"Take off your shoes and walk in your stocking feet," George suggested. But Bess paid no attention.

Suddenly, just ahead, a stone hunting lodge loomed up. Riggi suggested that Officer White and the two boys surround the building while the girls knocked on the door. No one came to answer.

A feeling of panic overtook Nancy. Ned just had to be in here. She cried out loudly, "Ned! Ned Nickerson! Are you in there?"

She listened intently. No sound came from inside. Finally she shouted again. Then she listened. Her pulse quickened. Had she heard a noise, or were her ears playing tricks on her?

"No, I'm right!" she said aloud. "Listen, everybody!"

There was a muffled cry from inside the building. *"Help!"*

CHAPTER VI

The Rescue

"Iт's Ned!" Nancy cried. "We must get in at once!"

Officer Riggi ran to her side. "Just a minute. This may be a ruse," he told her. "We don't want any more captures. I suggest that you girls stay here. We men will break in and see what's going on."

"All right," Nancy conceded, although she chafed under the restraint.

Bess and George hurried over to her and Bess said, "Oh, I hope it's Ned and he's all right!"

The others did not comment. They waited breathlessly as the two policemen forced open a window and climbed into the hunting lodge. In a few seconds the front door opened and Riggi called out, "Come in!"

"You go first," Burt suggested to Nancy.

She fairly leaped inside. The two officers had

just whipped a pillowcase from the head of a bound-up young man lying on the floor, his face pale, his dark, wavy hair disheveled.

"Ned!" Nancy cried and ran to his side.

"Boy, am I glad to see you all," he murmured weakly. Then he grinned. "I sure could use something to eat. Anybody bring along lunch?" This broke the long tension over Ned's absence.

The others burst into laughter and helped him to his feet. In a moment Ned's hands, which had been tied behind his back, were freed and his ankles unbound. He wavered a little as he tried to walk but Nancy supported him until he regained his equilibrium.

Bess opened her large handbag and brought out a box of crackers and a candy bar. She gave them to Ned, saying, "I always carry a little snack for emergency. I guess this is an emergency." She looked sideways at George as if expecting to be either teased or chided about her penchant for snacks, but her cousin said nothing.

"As soon as you feel like talking, Ned," said Officer White, "tell us what happened."

"But please make it snappy," Riggi added. "Your kidnappers will probably be back. It would be best if all you young people are away from here before their return."

It did not take Ned long to tell his story. He had been walking across the Emerson campus toward the library when a car with two men in it had stopped and the dark-complexioned driver had asked directions to the main gate.

"I walked over to tell them and a moment later a handkerchief with something sweet-smelling was put under my nose. The next thing I knew I woke up in a cabin."

Ned said that when he awakened, a tall well-built African black was standing over him. "He spoke very little English and said that his language was Swahili. He told me to call him Joe."

"Swahili Joe!" Nancy murmured excitedly to herself.

Ned quickly continued. "Joe was my guard and evidently felt he could manage me without my being bound up, so I wasn't tied and could walk around."

Ned grinned. "I didn't test his strength, but I did keep alert for some chance to escape. I discovered that there was a telephone in the cabin and once when Joe turned his back, I lifted the receiver to see if it was connected. There was a dial tone and this gave me the idea of trying to get in touch with you people."

Ned went on to say that while waiting for a chance to call, he figured out the latitude and longitude of the cabin's location by a mountain he could see in the distance. "It's where we go skiing sometimes."

"Nancy broke the 4182 code," Bess spoke up proudly.

Smiling his thanks, Ned continued his story. Joe had told him he was going outside for a minute, but that if Ned tried to escape he would get a good beating.

"So I didn't try it. Instead I dialed the number of our fraternity house. By the time you fellows came on the wire, I could hear Joe coming back, so I talked as fast as I could and hung up. Joe never suspected what I had done, because I was across the room by the time he came inside."

"Very clever," Officer Riggi put in. "And now I think you young folks should leave. White and I will stay here. Just two more questions before you go, though. Ned, do you know who your abductors were and what was the reason for the kidnapping?"

"I can answer your first question in the affirmative. My two abductors were a father and son from Mombasa, Africa. They are Indians. The father is Dhan, the son is named Jahan. They never talked so I have no idea why they kidnapped me. What little information I picked up about them came from Joe. I'm sure Nancy's involved, though, because Jahan and Dhan raced in and said you were coming. So the men moved me here."

By this time Ned had finished the box of crackers and eaten the candy bar. He declared he felt a hundred per cent better and would like to get back to Emerson. "I hope the dean will let me take the exam I missed. I'd hate to flunk the course."

Officer Riggi smiled. "If you have any trouble convincing him, just let me know."

"Thanks," said Ned.

After glasses of delicious water from a well just outside the lodge, the six young people started their trek back along the brook, past the cabin where Ned had first been taken, and on through the pear orchard to the road. By this time it was dusk. Fortunately the shots fired at the tires on Nancy's car had not punctured them. She slid behind the wheel while the others climbed in.

"I hope I can find my way back to Emerson," she said. "Ned, what's the latitude and longitude of your fraternity house?"

The others laughed. They knew that Nancy had a sixth sense for direction and did not need any instruction.

Silence had fallen over the group when Nancy spoke up. "Well, one mysterious disappearance solved."

"*One?* How many are there?" Bess asked.

"Have you been keeping something from us, Miss Drew?" George put in.

Nancy's friends had quickly discerned from the tone of her voice that there was indeed more mystery in the wind!

The girl detective revealed the curious story of

the two spider sapphires and a definite connection between that mystery and Ned's kidnapping.

"You mean, in other words, that our African holiday is going to be a really *hot* one!" Ned quipped.

Nancy merely smiled. It was dark by the time they reached the Longview Motel. Ned immediately telephoned his parents and told of the rescue. Nancy in turn called her father and asked him to notify the Faynes and Marvins.

When Nancy and Ned rejoined the others, Bess said, "I hope the dining room is still open. It's been a long time since lunch."

To their relief, dinner was still being served. "I'll have roast turkey with all the trimmings," Bess announced as they sat down.

When they had finished dessert, Ned remarked, "This day certainly didn't turn out the way I planned. There's a concert tonight at the university and a reception afterward for the soloist. She's an African black by the name of Madame Lilia Bulawaya. I understand she has a marvelous voice." He looked at his wrist watch. "Would you girls like to go? We'd be late but we could hear part of the concert."

Nancy asked, "Do you feel up to it, Ned?"

"Of course. Let's go! I guess you girls will want to change your clothes. Suppose we fellows go back to the fraternity house and make ourselves presentable. May I borrow your car, Nancy?"

"Go ahead. We'll be ready by the time you get back."

Nancy was dressed before the boys returned and put in a telephone call to State Police headquarters near Landsdowne. The officer who answered said he had little to report. The two prisoners had refused to talk. Jahan and Dhan had not appeared at the hunting lodge yet.

"We did get one little clue," the officer stated. "Our men found a letter on the floor of the prisoners' car. It was written to 'Dear Joe,' postmarked Mombasa, and was in Swahili. Unfortunately there was no return address and no signature."

"So the strong man was probably from Mombasa!" Nancy thought. Aloud she said, "Thank you for the information."

By this time the boys had arrived. Nancy quickly told them about the police report, then the young people set off for the concert. Madame Lilia Bulawaya was an outstanding performer. Not only was her voice sweet but she had a charming personality.

In her repertoire were several delightful songs in Swahili. She announced that she was singing these in honor of the Emerson student safari to Africa. When she finished, the applause was thunderous.

"Isn't she lovely?" Nancy said. "I'm so glad we'll have a chance to meet her later."

When the concert was over, there was a long reception line. On it were Professor and Mrs. Stanley who were to head the safari.

While Nancy stood in line waiting, she began to hum one of the Swahili songs. When she was introduced to Madame Bulawaya, the woman's eyes sparkled. "Didn't I hear you humming one of the songs I sang?"

Nancy nodded. "It is lovely. What do the words mean?"

"It's a lullaby. My mother used to sing it to us children. Would you like to learn the words?"

"Indeed I would," Nancy answered.

"Then as soon as I have met everyone, I will teach them to you," the singer said. "I'll meet you at that table where the bouquet of carnations is."

She turned to shake hands with the next person in line and Nancy moved off. She was thrilled by Madame Bulawaya's offer and waited for the singer to come. It was not long.

"Shall we first hum the melody together?" the woman asked.

Nancy was embarrassed but followed the suggestion.

"You have a very sweet voice and well-suited to singing in Swahili," Madame Bulawaya said. "You probably noticed that the language has a soft, musical quality."

It did not take long to learn the strange words of the lullaby. Nancy sang it softly phrase by phrase after Madame Bulawaya. Then the artist asked her to try it all the way through alone.

Nancy did so and the woman smiled. "You are an apt pupil," she said. "Now let us sing it together."

Nancy looked at Madame Bulawaya in astonishment. She was to sing the song with this great artist!

As she demurred, George spoke up. "Go ahead, Nancy. You can do it."

Madame Bulawaya smiled. "Of course you can."

She began singing and nodded for Nancy to make a duet of it. Finally she did and this time the voices were loud enough to be heard throughout the reception room. At the end everyone clapped and Nancy's face turned red with embarrassment.

Ned came dashing across the room. "That was great," he said. "Thank you so much, Madame Bulawaya, for teaching the song to Nancy. Now when we go to Africa, we'll get her to sing it once in a while."

Nancy laughed. "You'll do nothing of the kind," she told him. "I might just sing it for the six of us, but don't you ever dare ask me to do it in public!"

Ned merely grinned and made no comment. Bess spoke up and told the singer that Nancy had many talents. "She's a marvelous detective along with other things."

Madame Bulawaya looked amazed. "A detective? Then maybe you would do something for me while you're in Africa."

"I'll do anything I can," Nancy replied. "What is it you wish?"

Sadly the woman said that the song Nancy had learned was a favorite of a brother of hers named Tizam. "Once in a while he acted as a guide on a safari. About a year ago he took some white tourists from the United States into lion country. Tizam suddenly disappeared and the others thought he had been attacked and killed by a lioness."

"How dreadful!" said Nancy.

"Recently," Madame Bulawaya went on, "I had a dream that my brother is still alive. I'm making this concert tour to get enough money to send an expedition out to find him."

She turned pleading eyes to Nancy and her friends. "Perhaps you can pick up a clue. I would be eternally grateful to you if you could find Tizam."

CHAPTER VII

A Warning

"I'LL do all I can to find your brother," Nancy assured Madame Bulawaya.

"Oh, thank you," the singer replied.

"Where did Tizam's safari start from?" Nancy asked.

"Nairobi."

Nancy told the woman this would be the first stop in her safari and she would make some inquiries. Madame Bulawaya gave a description of her brother. He was tall, slender, and very dark. The singer smiled. "He has a lovely smile. I miss him very much and wish you the best of luck in finding him for me."

In a short time the reception ended and good-bys were said to Madame Bulawaya. The boys escorted Nancy and her friends to the Longview Motel. Ned said that he had been in touch with the dean about the exam he had missed that morning. He had obtained permission to take it the following afternoon.

"In the meantime I'll have to catch a little shut-eye and do some heavy studying."

Nancy told him that the three girls would leave early the next morning. "We'll meet you boys at Kennedy Airport in New York two hours before take-off time."

"Perfect! We'll be seeing you day after tomorrow!"

Ned, Burt, and Dave departed and the girls went to bed. They were up early the following day and were among the first diners in the restaurant. Before leaving for River Heights, Nancy telephoned State Police headquarters near Landsdowne again.

"I want to find out if there is any news of Jahan and Dhan."

The report was discouraging. The two kidnappers had not returned to the hunting lodge and the man called Swahili Joe had not been there either.

When Nancy told this to her friends, Bess burst out, "That horrible Joe! He left Ned there to starve!"

"Maybe not," George spoke up. "Swahili Joe may have been coming back when he discovered Ned had been rescued. In fact, he could have been the one to tell Jahan and Dhan that they'd better flee."

A little while later the three girls were on their way to River Heights. They discussed the problem of what clothes to take to Africa so they would have enough but not be overweight in their baggage.

Later Nancy talked it over with Hannah Gruen. "I don't want to pay a big charge for excess pounds going overseas."

The housekeeper smiled. "I'll help you avoid it. You put out everything you want to take and I'll weigh them on the bathroom scale."

Nearly all the next day was spent sorting, picking out, discarding. As the afternoon wore on, Nancy, tired of this job, began to talk about the two mysteries she was going to try solving in Africa.

"They both sound dangerous," Mrs. Gruen remarked. "But if I had to make a choice, I'd take the spider sapphire. Going into lion country after Mr. Tizam sounds really scary to me."

Nancy's eyes twinkled. "It might be exciting."

"Too exciting," the housekeeper said. Then she shrugged and put an arm around Nancy. "All I can say for the millionth time is, 'Please be careful.' "

At last the packing was finished. Late in the afternoon Mr. Drew drove Nancy, Bess, and George to the River Heights Airport where they were to board a plane for New York. He smiled fondly at them. "You know, I'm really envious.

Your trip sounds like a lot more fun than staying in my law office working on briefs."

Nancy hugged him. "If I hit a snag, I'll cable you to come and join us." She gave him a wink. "Shall I make the opportunity?"

"I'll let you know," he countered.

The plane to New York was announced over the loudspeaker and the girls climbed aboard. An hour later they reached Kennedy Airport in New York. Ned, Burt, and Dave were already there with the Stanleys. The professor was of medium height and had graying hair. He was very serious-looking in contrast to his plump, smiling wife.

"Madame Bulawaya told me, Nancy, that you're going to try locating her brother," Aunt Millie said. "I love mysteries." She chuckled. "Call on me if you need any help."

"I surely will."

Other members of the safari group arrived in twos and fours. Nancy and her friends knew all the boys but had never met any of the girls who were going along.

One tall, slender blond stood out in the group. She was overdressed for traveling, and it was quite evident that she wore a blond wig. Gwen Taylor met the others in a rather supercilious way and almost at once nobody seemed to care for her.

"She looks like a freak!" George whispered.

Bess came to Gwen's defense. "Maybe she's just shy and underneath it she's a nice person."

Her cousin did not agree. "She's too artificial."

There was a long wait before plane take-off, so Nancy and Ned walked around the airport building, looking for Jahan and Dhan. It was possible that if the men had not left the country, they had followed the young people and would try to cause them harm again. The couple saw nothing of the Indians, however, and returned to their group in the main lobby.

At that moment a voice came over the loud-speaker "Message for Miss Nancy Drew. Please come to your airline ticket office."

Nancy had jumped from her seat. She hoped that the message was not bad news from home. Ned went with her to the ticket office.

"Miss Drew?" a clerk asked.

When she nodded, he said that Nancy was to telephone her father immediately. He himself put the call through and the lawyer came on the wire.

"Nancy, don't worry. Everything is all right here. But I'm not so sure it will be all right for you in Africa. I want you to watch your step very carefully. Our police got a tip that Jahan and Dhan took off for Africa. They haven't been apprehended because apparently they were using passports under assumed names."

"Where did they go?" Nancy asked.

"The police haven't received a reply yet from the immigration authorities on this point. I thought I should warn you, though. I know it's almost take-off time, so run along. Hannah sends her love and of course you have mine, and promise me you won't go anywhere alone."

"I promise, Dad, and don't worry. I aim to solve both mysteries without being kidnapped." She laughed gaily to reassure her father, then said good-by.

Before long, the chattering, laughing Emerson group hurried aboard the chartered plane. When they were airborne, small groups began singing songs, some of them college numbers, others from musical comedy hits. Once in a while someone would call out a wisecrack and set everyone laughing.

"This is such fun," said Bess to Nancy.

The three girls were seated together. Ned, Burt, and Dave were across the aisle. Dinner was served and presently lights were turned low and everyone was expected to sleep. The young people were in too exuberant a mood for sleep and it was past midnight before they settled down.

At three A.M. New York time the voices of the stewardesses could be heard saying, "Good morning! Would you care for some orange juice?"

The Emersonians blinked open one eye, confused for the moment as to where they were. But presently they sat up and drank the juice. Rolls, scrambled eggs, and a beverage followed.

"I'm still confused and sleepy," said Bess. "What time is it?"

George giggled. "Which country will you have it in? In London where we're heading it's eight A.M."

Nancy told Bess there would be time for a nap later. The safari schedule included a day's stop at a motel near the airport. "You can sleep for a few hours, Bess."

Ned's group arranged to meet in the lobby at lunchtime. Nancy arrived ahead of the others and decided to put a question to the desk clerk.

"I'm sure you have many Indians from Africa stopping at your motel, but the group I'm with is looking for two special gentlemen. I wonder if by any chance they may have stopped here."

"What are their names?" the man asked.

"Jahan and Dhan."

The clerk consulted his list of recent guests, then shook his head. "No men by those names have been here."

Nancy was about to walk off when it occurred to her that if the men were using passports with fictitious names, they naturally would have had to use these.

She said to the clerk, "The men may be traveling incognito," and gave a full description of the father and son.

The clerk smiled. "I believe your friends have been here, but they've gone."

"To Nairobi?" Nancy queried.

The man at the desk shrugged. "Or possibly Mombasa," he said. "At least that is where the Prasads are from."

Nancy thanked him for the information and walked off. "So Prasad is the name Jahan and Dhan used on their passports!" she thought.

Soon her friends came downstairs.

"Boy, did I sleep!" Burt burst out.

Everyone admitted having slept well and all had ravenous appetites. In the dining room they were seated at a table for six. Bess ordered two kinds of fruit, soup, baked fish, and a whipped cream dessert.

"If all you do is sit in a plane and sleep and eat, they're going to charge you for being overweight," George teased her.

Bess endeavored to defend herself and finally told the waitress she would skip dessert.

As dusk came on, Professor and Mrs. Stanley gathered the members of the safari and engaged taxis to take them to the airport. Although the group was as merry as on the previous evening's flight, the gaiety did not last so long. By ten-thirty everyone was sound asleep.

Nancy did not know how much later it was

when she was suddenly awakened by all the lights being turned on brightly.

In a moment the captain's voice came over the loudspeaker. "Please fasten your seat belts! Turbulence ahead! I repeat, please fasten your seat belts immediately!"

The sleepy students did so almost automatically. They wondered why the order had been given because the plane seemed to be rushing through the night without trouble.

The stillness was abruptly shattered by Gwen Taylor exclaiming, "I hate seat belts! They make me positively ill! I'm not going to put mine on!"

She was defiantly standing in the aisle when the plane made a sickening drop. Gwen grabbed the back of the seat and eased herself down.

A few moments later the plane began to roll sharply to left and right. The craft sank again as if it had suddenly lost all of its lift. This time the plane seemed to be going completely out of control. Tensely the passengers clutched the armrests of their seats.

CHAPTER VIII

The Lemur Cage

ALTHOUGH everyone became more alarmed as the plane continued to lose altitude, they all managed to remain quiet except Gwen Taylor.

Again she stood up in the aisle. Her friend Hal Harper tried his best to make her sit down but she refused.

"If I'm going to be killed," she exclaimed, "it's going to be standing up, not tied to a seat!"

She pitched forward and almost fell. Hal grabbed her and pushed the hysterical girl into her own seat.

At the same moment the pilot's voice came clearly over the loudspeaker. "Will the young lady who is standing up please stay in her seat and put on her belt? This is an order from your captain."

Gwen did not adjust the seat belt, but she was quiet for several seconds. Then suddenly she got up again and lurched forward. "I'm going to have my father sue this airline!" she cried out.

Within seconds she had yanked open the door to the pilot's compartment, bolted inside, and slammed the door. Hal Harper unfastened his own belt and started after her.

From the rear of the cabin the steward yelled frantically, "Sit down! Put on your belt!"

As Hal obeyed, there came a scream from the pilot's compartment. The next moment the plane went into a dive!

Those in the cabin held their breath, but the pilot seemed to be a magician. No matter how violently his craft was tossed about, he seemed able to get it back under control.

The plane climbed rapidly and in a few moments leveled out in smooth air. Everyone uttered groans of relief, then turned their eyes toward the door of the pilot's cabin. What was going on inside?

Presently the door flew open. Gwen came out, looking very disheveled. Her wig was awry, giving her a comical look.

As Gwen half stumbled toward her own seat, Bess called out, "What made you scream, Gwen?"

The unruly girl stopped short and said haughtily, "If you must know, the flight engineer grabbed me."

Bess's eyes lighted up. "How exciting!"

"Well—uh—I screamed because I didn't think this was quite fair to Hal," Gwen said lamely.

George burst into laughter. "Better straighten

your wig, Gwen, or Hal won't love you any more."

In disdain Gwen quickly pulled her false hair into place and went to her seat.

"For Pete's sake," said Hal, "what were you up to?"

"I was trying to put some sense into that pilot's head," Gwen answered defiantly.

Nancy, Bess, and George exchanged glances and George remarked, "Do we have to put up with that pain on this whole trip?"

Nancy grinned. "How would you like to try changing her?"

"No thanks. I'll leave that to you and Bess. You're better at that sort of thing than I am."

Aunt Millie Stanley came forward and stood beside Gwen. "I'm terribly sorry you were so frightened," she said. "I guess everyone was. Do you feel all right now?"

"Yes, thank you. I lost my head. Sorry."

The Emerson students and their friends went back to sleep. A few hours later the pilot announced that they were approaching Nairobi.

When the group entered the airport building, Nancy looked around to see if Jahan and Dhan might be spying on them. As she and Ned waited in line to go through Immigration and Customs, she said, "I have a feeling we're being followed."

Ned grinned. "Don't let your imagination run away with you." Then he said seriously, "I guess you and I had better be on our guard at all times."

There was no sign of the two Indians here or at the attractive hotel where the group was to stay. The Stanleys announced that they were all to meet in an hour for a bus tour of the city.

Nancy found the trip fascinating. The Emerson group was divided among three buses that were painted with black and white zebra-like stripes. The buses were camouflaged so that when traveling in wild animal country, from a distance they would look like a small herd of zebras.

The bustling city of three hundred and fifteen thousand inhabitants was international in character. There were white people, blacks, coloreds— which were a combination of black and some other race—Arabs, and Indians.

"Don't you love the Indians' native dress?" Bess asked Dave.

"They sure are colorful," he replied, "but I'd just as soon wear American-type clothes."

The men wore white turbans and a fringe of beard, but English business suits. The women's saris were made of several layers of veil-thin pastel materials. Scarfs covered their hair. Some of the women had a jewel embedded in their foreheads.

In contrast the Arab women were somberly swathed in black. Some had the lower part of their faces covered.

Professor Stanley, who was seated in the front of the bus, arose from time to time and gave statistics about the city. He said that the Arabs and Indians spoke their own languages and English. The blacks spoke Swahili.

"Some of them have learned English and for this reason are able to obtain better jobs."

The bus stopped in front of a Moslem mosque. To reach it one had to cross a long flagstone pavement. A guard told the group that they must remove their shoes before walking on it.

George exclaimed, "Ouch! These stones are boiling hot!"

Nancy grinned. "Don't forget we're not far from the equator."

The inside of the building was like a large lobby with niches and a place for the priest to stand. In one corner a man lay asleep on the floor. When Burt expressed surprise at this, a guard said that all Moslems were welcome to come in out of the midday heat and take a nap.

Back in the bus again, Professor Stanley told the students, "It is believed that the Arabs were the first foreigners to set foot on African soil. They went pretty far inland and became traders. It is through them that African art was brought to the outside world."

After a restful lunch and a short stroll, the young tourists were ready to start on a trip to Nairobi National Park, a wildlife game preserve.

Professor Stanley announced, "All the animals

roam loose. The park covers forty-four square miles and has twenty miles of roads."

The buses had barely entered the vast stretches of grassland when Bess exclaimed, "I see a giraffe! Wow, is he tall!" The animal stood higher than the tree from which it was eating the top leaves. "I've seen giraffes in zoos but never one that tall."

Burt laughed. "Maybe they come bigger in the open."

As they rode along, Nancy and her friends saw graceful eland, sturdy hartebeest, dignified maribou storks and ostriches. All the animals seemed friendly and unafraid. Several of them came close to the buses. The drivers turned off the road and started through a bumpy field.

"Oh, this is horrible!" Bess cried out. She was swaying from side to side and banged her elbow hard against the window. Dave put an arm around Bess to keep her steady.

"Where are we going?" she asked.

Professor Stanley turned around in his seat and called back, "Our driver has spotted some lions. It is against the rules to get out of the bus and should one of the beasts start toward us, close your windows immediately. Lions do not attack unless provoked, but one never knows what may provoke them."

George said in a low voice, "I wonder how Gwen likes all this."

The driver pulled around a small clump of high bushes near a tiny stream and stopped. He spoke to Professor Stanley, who in turn called out in a loud whisper, "It is advisable that we do not talk. It might disturb the lions. If you will look ahead in a grassy depression near the water you will see a lion family. Papa is stretched out asleep. By the way, Papa sleeps seventeen out of the twenty-four hours every day."

Ned grinned. "No time to be the aggressor."

Professor Stanley smiled. "Not normally. The lioness does the killing for food and drags the antelope or gazelle back to Papa. He is the first to eat. After he has gorged himself, Mama eats her share. The cubs take what is left."

By this time everyone was standing up and training their eyes hard on the area Professor Stanley had indicated. Presently the lion raised his head and looked sleepily at the bus.

"What a regal creature he is!" Nancy whispered.

The others agreed. Suddenly they saw something moving a little nearer the water.

"The cubs!" Nancy said.

The next moment she spotted their mother, who also seemed to be sleeping. Professor Stanley said that no doubt the whole family had just finished a big good meal.

The other two buses pulled in nearby. Gwen Taylor poked her head and shoulders far out of a window and pointed her camera at the beasts. The lion raised its head again and this time gave a loud roar. The noise unnerved Gwen and she dropped her camera.

"Oh!" she screamed. "Somebody get my camera!"

Professor Stanley called across to her, "It's against the rules for anyone to get out of the bus in lion country."

Gwen became petulant. "That camera is very special. It cost a great deal of money. I'm going to get it back."

"Stay where you are!" the professor said sternly.

The driver of the bus Gwen was in refused to open the door. The girl protested so loudly that the commotion disturbed the animals. Both the lion and lioness stood up and looked balefully at the visitors.

"We'd better leave," Professor Stanley told their driver. He called across to the other two drivers to do the same.

Mrs. Stanley, who was in the bus with Gwen, said she would try to rescue the camera. She had brought along an umbrella with a curved handle. With it she reached out the window and caught a leather strap attached to the camera. In moments she retrieved Gwen's property. The buses backed up, turned around, and went on to other sections of the park.

George was extremely annoyed by Gwen's actions. "If I were running this tour, I'd make her go home."

"Oh, she'll probably change," Bess prophesied.

When the buses reached the hotel, Professor Stanley announced that the Emerson safari had been invited to supper at the home of an American couple, Mr. and Mrs. Northrup. Everyone was to be ready to leave at six o'clock.

The Northrup home was situated on the outskirts of the city. It was a large English-type house, set in a beautiful tiered garden. Huge poinsettia plants, two stories high, grew against the walls. All the other flowers in the garden were of massive size. An attractive swimming pool was ringed with bright-red and white hibiscus.

The Northrups were a charming couple. Their host was connected with the American Embassy in Nairobi and related many interesting stories about this former British Protectorate, now being governed entirely by blacks.

The visitors divided into groups. Mrs. Northrup took Nancy and her friends down to the lowest terrace to show them a pet lemur. The animal paced back and forth in a small, barred cage.

"It's an intriguing-looking animal," Nancy remarked. "It has a face like a fox, a body like a cat, and a long, ringed, striped tail."

"The only place in the world where there are lemurs is on the island of Madagascar," Mrs. Northrup told her guests.

The Americans stayed for several minutes to watch the animal. Then all of them except Nancy went back up the steps to the house. She was too fascinated by the pet to leave.

"I'd love to own one of these," she thought. "But I suppose it would be cruel to—"

Nancy's thoughts were suddenly blotted out when a sack was pulled down over her head and quickly tied around her neck. As Nancy tried to grab her attacker, a piece of paper was thrust into her hand. Then she heard running footsteps.

Nancy began to suffocate. She realized that the sack was lined with plastic. She must get it off at once! But this was impossible. The knots which held the cord tight were firmly tied. Nancy knew that in a moment she would black out!

CHAPTER IX

Baboon Thief

FRANTICALLY Nancy tore at the cords which held the plastic-lined sack over her head. She could not do without air much longer, but her struggles to free herself were in vain.

"I must get help!" she thought wildly.

Feeling as if her lungs were ready to burst, Nancy stumbled toward the steps of the terrace. Then she collapsed to the ground. The next moment she felt hands working at the knots and the sack was ripped from her head.

"Nancy, whatever happened?" she vaguely heard Ned say.

Then, dazedly, she realized that he was massaging her back and she was gulping in fresh air. Nancy was still too weak to open her eyes, but she could hear Ned's voice as if coming from a far distance.

"Nancy! Nancy! Wake up!" he pleaded.

Seconds later she opened her eyes.

"You all right now, Nancy?"

"Yes, I guess so," she answered softly.

Ned told her not to try talking until she felt stronger. Finally she was able to tell him what had happened.

"Who was the rat who did it?" he asked. His eyes blazed with anger.

"I don't know," Nancy replied. "I didn't see anyone. The sack was pulled over my head by someone who crept up behind me."

Just then she remembered the paper which had been thrust into her hand by the unknown assailant. She asked Ned to look for it.

He found the crumpled paper near the lemur's cage and brought it to where she was sitting on the grass. They looked at it together. Both gasped. The warning message read:

Nancy Drew: Give up the spider sapphire case or worse harm will come to you.

Ned stared at the paper a moment, then looked at Nancy fondly. "I agree with the writer about giving up the case."

Nancy did not reply at once. Finally she said, "Ned, you know I never give up on a mystery."

"But, Nancy, if anything should happen to you on this trip, how could I ever explain it to your father?"

"But you wouldn't be responsible," Nancy countered.

Ned looked directly at her. "Leaving all that aside, I personally don't want anything to happen to you. Hereafter I'm going to stay close to you whether you want to be guarded or not."

"Thanks. With you nearby I know I'll be safe," she said with a smile. "Well, I feel all right now. Let's go back up to the party."

Nancy brushed her dress. Then she tidied her hair with a comb from her purse, which had not been disturbed by her attacker.

The couple walked up the steps. As they reached the top terrace, they were met by their friends. George inquired why Nancy had not joined them. When they heard what had happened, Bess, George, Burt, and Dave became alarmed.

"It seems," said Bess, "as if you aren't safe anywhere, Nancy. Somebody must be following you every minute, waiting for a chance to harm you."

Nancy smiled and said, "I hereby appoint all of you as my bodyguards. Surely no one could get at me with you five brave people surrounding me."

George grinned. "Not with us facing outward at all times!"

Bess looked at Ned. "I think we'd better put you inside the ring too. I haven't forgotten yet that you were kidnapped and left to starve."

Nancy noticed Mr. and Mrs. Northrup coming

toward them. "Let's not say anything to them about what happened," she begged, and the others nodded.

"I'm fascinated by your lemur," Nancy told the couple. "Did you bring it from Madagascar?"

"No, a friend brought it. She travels a great deal. She is particularly keen on safaris."

This gave Nancy an idea. "By any chance have you or your friend ever heard of a guide named Tizam?"

Mrs. Northrup looked surprised. "Did you know him?"

"No," Nancy replied, "but I had the pleasure of meeting his sister Madame Lilia Bulawaya. We heard her sing at Emerson College and she told us about her brother."

Mrs. Northrup said that her friend, Mrs. Munger, had mentioned the sad fate of the guide. "The story is he was attacked by a lion."

"Yes," Nancy answered, "but Tizam's sister believes he may still be alive. She asked us to try to find out what we can while we're traveling around Kenya."

"Would you like to meet Mrs. Munger and learn more about what happened on the safari?" Mrs. Northrup asked.

"Yes, indeed," Nancy replied.

Mrs. Northrup offered to telephone her friend immediately and make an appointment.

"Our group," said Nancy, "is leaving tomorrow

morning for Treetops Inn. We'll be staying there overnight. May we see Mrs. Munger when we come back?"

"I'll try to arrange a meeting two days from now," Mrs. Northrup said. She went off to telephone but soon returned. "Mrs. Munger has invited you and your friends to tea that day." Nancy thanked her for making the arrangements.

A few hours later she and the others said good-by to the Northrups, thanking them for their delightful hospitality. Everyone slept soundly and was up early for the next part of their safari. All of them looked forward to staying at Treetops Inn, built into the branches of enormous fig trees. From there, they would watch wild animals come to the nearby water hole.

The drive was long and hot. A stop was made at the Outspan Hotel, where they had lunch and deposited their main baggage in a large room. Only flight bags were allowed to be carried for their overnight stay at Treetops.

In the middle of the afternoon, the three black-and-white-striped buses traveled up a winding road through a woods and came to a halt at a fence. Everyone climbed out and a tall gate was opened for the visitors. Some little distance beyond stood a man in a belted khaki suit, a stout rifle slung over one shoulder.

"This is Mr. Zucker, our White Hunter," Professor Stanley called out.

"Please form a circle," said the man, who had a broad British accent.

The Emerson group gathered in front of him.

"We have between quarter and half a mile to walk to reach the inn. I must caution all of you to be as quiet as possible. Otherwise you will scare away the animals."

Bess, looking nervously at the rifle, asked him, "Do you have to use that very often?"

"Not often." The hunter held out the rifle to show that it was larger than the type usually carried by hunters. "This is the only rifle," he said, "which can pierce the hide of a rhino or an elephant."

"You mean they attack sometimes?" Bess queried.

"Sometimes. Keep your eyes open, and again I ask all of you not to talk. When we reach the inn, you are to go up the stairway and remain inside the building until tomorrow morning. It would be too dangerous for you to be on the grounds."

George glanced at Gwen Taylor. Hal had hold of her arm and was whispering into her ear. No doubt he was reassuring her and warning the girl to do exactly as she had been told.

The hunter turned and the Emersonians followed him in silence. Their eyes darted to the partly grassy, partly wooded area on either side of the path. They saw nothing scary—merely timid gazelles.

Treetops Inn was the most unusual hotel Nancy and her friends had ever seen. There were extra supports besides the tree trunks to hold the weight of the large building. A small wooden stairway led to the first floor, leaving the ground area free for the animals to wander beneath.

The visitors were amazed at the size of the place. There was a center section containing a lobby, a lounge, and a large dining room. To left and right were corridors and here and there a tree branch blocked the path, forcing guests to climb over it to continue down the hallway. The inn had two stories, with long porches on both levels and an observation roof.

As soon as the girls had been assigned rooms, they took their cameras and went to the lower porch. In front of it was a large water hole. Professor Stanley, walking by, told them it was saline and this was one reason the animals came there to drink. The girls chose front-row seats a little distance from one end of the porch.

"Look who's here," George whispered.

Seated in a wicker chair at the very end of the porch was Gwen Taylor. Next to her was a wooden partition which separated the porch from the front bedroom area. She was alone and was reading a book which lay on her lap. Apparently Gwen had no interest in the animals that came to the water hole.

The baboon snatched off Gwen's wig

"She's probably sulking because Hal scolded her," George guessed.

At that moment two warthogs appeared from among the trees. They went directly toward the water, but instead of drinking it and retreating, they waddled in.

"Ugh!" Bess said.

"That's how they clean themselves," George said in a whisper.

Nancy was amazed at the silence of the place. Not only the people on the porches, but the beasts that came to the water hole were very quiet. Each breed of animal waited until the ones already there had finished drinking or bathing.

A group of wildebeest had just left, when Nancy said in a low voice, "Get your cameras ready! Here come some water buffalo."

George grinned. "They have bowed hind legs!"

The girls' attention was distracted by a baboon which scampered along the railing in front of them. It stopped briefly to grab candy from Bess's hand.

Then it went on to where Gwen still sat reading. He gazed at her a moment, then Nancy saw one of his great arms suddenly reach out. In a moment he had snatched off Gwen's wig!

"Oh!" she screamed.

Gwen tried to grab the hair piece but the baboon drew back and slapped her arm. The next moment he scooted up the side of the building, carrying the wig with him.

Nancy leaned out to look up and saw that the animal was seated on the railing of the flat roof. She jumped out of her chair, dashed through the lobby of the inn, and up an outside stairway that led to the top of the building. No one was there. The baboon was swishing the wig back and forth across the floor.

"He'll ruin it!" Nancy thought.

She hurried forward, but just before reaching the animal, he jumped to the railing and scooted to the far side of the roof. As Nancy dashed after him, he raised his upper lip, baring his teeth. She knew now that the only way to get the hair piece away from the baboon was to use kindness and coaxing.

Nancy took a piece of candy from her handbag and held it in the palm of her hand. The baboon looked at it, then turned back to the wig and began pulling the hair from it.

Nancy laid the candy on the railing and waited. Quick as a flash the baboon ran toward it, grabbed it in his mouth, and ran off without dropping the wig. The next moment he jumped toward a tree and started downward.

CHAPTER X

A Doubtful Robbery

NANCY could reach neither the baboon nor the wig. All she could do was try some strategy.

"Nice boy!" she called to him in a soft voice. "I shan't hurt you. Come on over here."

The animal eyed her without flinching and did not move. Then, as if trying to tease her, he reached up and hung the wig on a high branch of the tree.

At that moment a waiter came up the stairs carrying a tray of pineapple slices, cookies, and teacups. He was followed by a man with the tea service. Behind him walked the White Hunter with his rifle. He stationed himself at the far end of the roof, while the waiters set the food down on a long table.

"Tea, miss?" one of the waiters asked Nancy.

"Not now, thank you," she replied, "but is it against the rule to feed the baboons?"

"Oh no."

"Then may I have a couple of cookies for my friend up there in the tree?"

A waiter handed some to her and she walked over to the railing. Nancy called to the baboon, "Cookies in exchange for the wig!"

The animal did not comply. He jumped to the railing and put out a hand for a cookie.

"First go get that wig," she said, holding back.

The baboon had other ideas. With a quick swoop of his arm, he took the cookie out of her hand and jumped back to the tree.

Guests began to troop up the stairway. Bess and George appeared first, then the three boys.

"Where's the wig?" Bess asked.

Nancy pointed and said, "I have half a mind to jump over to that branch myself and get it."

The boys said that if anyone was going to get the wig, one of them would. Again the baboon outwitted them. Grabbing the hair piece in his hand, he scooted down the tree and out of sight.

George spoke up. "Who'd want to wear that now anyway?" she asked. "It's ruined and probably full of fleas!"

The others nodded but Bess said sympathetically, "I feel sorry for Gwen. That wig meant a lot to her."

"Too much," said George crisply.

"Someone will have to tell her," Nancy remarked. "As soon as I have a piece of this delicious-looking pineapple, I'll go do it."

"Please let me," Bess begged. "I have an idea what to say to her."

As soon as Bess had eaten, she excused herself and hurried off. She found Gwen in her room. It was evident she had been crying. Bess went up and put an arm about the distressed girl.

"Gwen, don't let an old baboon get you down. You know something?"

"What?" Gwen asked.

"It's foolish of you to let a hair piece spoil your whole safari. Gwen, you have beautiful dark hair and just between you and me it's a lot more becoming to the color of your eyes and skin than blond hair is. Tell you what! Let me shampoo and set your hair. I'll bet you'll love it—and Hal too."

Gwen looked at Bess for several seconds before she said, "I've been so horrible on this trip I don't see how anybody would want to bother with me."

Bess hugged her. "Don't be a silly, Gwen. You just be yourself and everybody will love you."

"You mean it?"

"Sure. I'll go for some shampoo I brought and we'll get to work."

Gwen smiled at her new-found friend. "Okay," she agreed. "You're a darling, Bess."

Up on the roof, Ned suddenly called out, "Here come the rhinos!"

"I can't say they're beautiful," George re-marked.

Nancy laughed. "Unless you make yourself be-lieve that everything in the world is beautiful."

The two-tusked, beady-eyed animals sauntered in and at once took charge. The White Hunter walked over and told the group that next to the lion, the rhinos are the most feared animal in the jungle.

"They're very powerful and mean," he said. "They've been known to turn over a bus!"

Nancy noticed that the rhinos seemed to stay in a family group. As they approached the water hole, all the warthogs, gazelles, wild pigs, and water buffalo left.

Presently Nancy detected a disturbance among the rhinos. A husband and wife seemed to be hav-ing an argument. Mama Rhino began to hiss and snort at him. He put up no resistance. Instead, he turned and walked toward the inn. There he began to cry piteously.

George chuckled. "The big sissy!"

Nancy grinned. "That's one of the funniest things I've ever seen. A great big fat dangerous rhino crying like a baby!"

Papa remained in the spot until Mama came for him. She chucked him in the neck with the longer of her two tusks. As if he had had sufficient punishment, she led the way back to the water hole. He followed meekly.

Hal Harper came to join the group. "Have any of you seen Gwen?" he asked. "She's been gone for ages."

Nancy's eyes twinkled. "She'll be here presently. Bess has her in tow."

"Why?"

"You'll see."

Suddenly a pleasant voice behind them said, "Hello, everybody! Here's a new Gwen! Done over by a big baboon and a girl named Bess Marvin."

The others turned and looked in astonishment. The old Gwen Taylor was gone. Here stood a beautiful, smiling girl with dark wavy hair becomingly arranged in a modern hairdo.

"Gwen!" Hal cried out and dashed forward. "You're absolutely stunning!" He gave her an affectionate hug. Gwen blushed, and as other compliments came her way, looked happily at the group.

George more than anyone else was taken aback by the transformation. She whispered to Nancy, "Gwen's positively ravishing."

Supper was announced and everyone went into the attractive rustic dining room with its long tables. In the center of each was a deep groove into which trays of food could be inserted and passed along. The Emerson boys and their friends became a bit noisy and Mr. Zucker was forced to ask for silence.

"We're hoping that elephants will come to the water hole tonight," he said. "But if you make too much noise, they may jolly well be discouraged."

The young people ate the delicious roast beef meal almost in silence.

After supper Nancy talked with Mrs. Zucker, the wife of the White Hunter. She in turn introduced the girl to two men guests.

"Miss Drew, I should like you to meet Messrs. Ramon and Sharma. They come from Mombasa. Miss Drew is from the States."

"Charmed to meet you," Ramon said, and Sharma added, "I am delighted to make your acquaintance."

Both men wore English-type sports clothes, but Ramon had a large, beautiful ruby ring on the first finger of his right hand.

He caught Nancy looking at it admiringly and said, "We Indians like precious stones. This ring has been in my family for many generations."

"It is handsome," said Nancy.

Sharma spoke up. "If you admire fine, precious gems, you ought to see the fabulous spider sapphire. But unfortunately it has disappeared."

"I've heard about it," Nancy replied. "I understand it was stolen."

The two Indians exchanged glances, then Ramon said, "Perhaps, but I doubt it."

Nancy asked what made him think this.

Ramon smiled and said, "Oh, just personal reasons. But, Miss Drew, please do not put any credence in my—what you Americans call hunch."

She merely smiled. It was an amazing coincidence that she herself had had the same hunch, but she did not mention this to the Indian.

The conversation ended when the White Hunter came to announce that elephants were arriving at the water hole. All the guests hurried to the porches. The large lumbering beasts appeared from the woods and lined up in front of Treetops.

"Why don't they go to the water hole?" Nancy whispered to Mr. Zucker, who was standing next to her.

"They are afraid of the rhinos. They will stand here and wait patiently until the other animals go away."

The interested watchers seated on the porch chairs did not mind the wait. It gave them a chance to take flashlight pictures of the great animals.

After a while George became restless. She got up and began pacing back and forth behind the chairs. As George reached the far end of the porch, she became fascinated by a dark shape climbing up the side of the building.

"It looks like a baboon," George said to herself. "But they're not usually out at night."

She went near the railing and watched, fascinated. Yes, it was a huge baboon. Perhaps she should return to her chair.

Before George could back away, the beast grabbed her and pulled her onto the railing! George was in a panic. Did he intend to drop her to the ground? She could be seriously injured—perhaps killed!

George struggled to free herself, but the baboon's grip was like iron. Was this the same animal which had taken the wig? Was he just being playful?

George decided not. She tried to cry out for help but a great paw was clamped over her mouth.

The helpless girl was swung from the railing and quickly taken to the ground. The baboon ran off with her toward the woods!

CHAPTER XI

Jungle Clue

"WHERE's George?" asked Burt, walking up to Nancy and Ned. He had gone inside the inn to get more film.

"Why, I don't know," Nancy replied, looking along the dark porch. "Last I noticed she was walking up and down."

The group continued to watch the elephants. The rhinos had left and now the big beasts went to the water hole to suck up the saline water through their trunks.

"Aren't their babies cute?" said Bess, shooting a flash-bulb picture of two who had waded into the hole with their mother and were spraying water over their backs.

Presently Nancy became uneasy over George. Quietly she left her chair and searched throughout the inn for her friend. George was not in sight.

"Is it possible she disobeyed the White Hunter's orders, went down the steps, and onto the ground?" Nancy thought worriedly. She came back and mentioned it to her friends.

Bess spoke up in defense of her cousin. "George wouldn't do such a foolish thing," she said.

Her friends agreed but wondered why she had disappeared. Nancy decided they had better tell the White Hunter. They found him talking to his wife.

"This is serious," he said. "I will go downstairs and take a look." Swinging his rifle over a shoulder, he hurried off.

Just as he reached the top of the stairs, he met George coming up. The White Hunter said sternly:

"It is the rule here that no one leave these premises."

"Please, Mr. Zucker," George pleaded, "I didn't go of my own will. Let me tell my story."

She went into the lounge, and when everyone was seated, related how the baboon had carried her over the railing and down to the ground. "Then he ran off with me."

Bess gave a cry of dismay. "That's horrible! How did you get away?"

George said that when they were a little distance from Treetops, suddenly the baboon had begun to talk.

"I couldn't understand him, but I knew then

that he was a man in disguise and not a baboon."

Burt's face was livid. He declared that he was going out and "find that human beast and give him what he deserves."

Mr. Zucker put a stop to this idea at once. "It would be extremely dangerous," he said. "The jungle is alive at night with preying animals. You might easily be a victim."

George looked at Burt. "Thanks a lot. But since I'm safe, let's call it quits."

"Tell us how you got loose," Nancy begged.

George said that as soon as she realized the baboon was a man in disguise, an idea came to her. If the headpiece were twisted, he would not be able to see.

"So I gave it a sudden yank sideways. He was so surprised, he let go of me. I ran back here as fast as I could."

"Thank goodness you are safe," Mrs. Zucker said. "George, can you remember any of the words the man said to you?"

"I don't think he was talking to me," George replied. "He seemed to be muttering to himself." She thought a moment, then repeated a few of the words she could remember.

"That's Swahili," Mrs. Zucker said. " '*Glw a heri*' means good-by."

The White Hunter said to his wife, "Do you remember that man from Mombasa who was a

combination strong man and acrobat in the traveling circus?"

Mrs. Zucker nodded. "You mean the one they
called Swahili Joe?"

Nancy and her friends were startled when they
heard the name. If the man in baboon disguise
had been Swahili Joe, then he had followed the
young people to Treetops and intended to harm
them.

"Tell us more about him," Nancy requested.

Mr. Zucker said that Swahili Joe had been a
fine person and an excellent performer. "Unfortunately he had a bad fall and it was reported he was
not well coordinated after that and had to leave
the circus."

Nancy thought, "Then he'd take orders from
Jahan and Dhan, not realizing what harm he's
doing."

"I wish I had seen this baboon fellow," said
Ned. "He and I would have recognized each
other."

Professor and Mrs. Stanley had heard rumors of
George's absence and now came to learn more
about it. They were thunderstruck and alarmed
by the story.

"I had no idea," said Aunt Millie, "that this
trip would involve any of you in so much danger."

"I know it's all my fault," Nancy spoke up.
"I'm dreadfully sorry."

George came to Nancy's defense. "You had nothing to do with that baboon man coming here and carting me off."

Nancy was unconvinced. She had felt for some time that to hunt for her enemies would not be necessary because they would come after her.

"Maybe I should take the initiative," she thought, but did not express this idea aloud for fear of alarming the others.

Bess could see that Nancy was upset. To dispel the tenseness of the situation, she said, "O to be an elephant, with no worries!"

"That's where you're wrong," Professor Stanley told her. "Did you ever hear what happens to the ex-leaders of herds?"

Bess shook her head. The professor went on, "When a bull elephant becomes old, and a young buck wants to become the leader, he fights his way to the top and forces the old fellow out. No one in the herd dares come to his defense. It seems to be the law and nobody breaks it."

"What happens to the poor old elephant that's out of a job?" Bess asked.

Professor Stanley said that he had to become a lone wanderer. "They often grieve so much that they don't eat and starve to death."

"Oh!" Bess exclaimed. "That whole system is very cruel."

"Nature," said the professor, "often does seem cruel. But we must remember the natural laws which bring about a balance of life on this earth. If there weren't such a thing, the whole world would be in chaos."

He stopped speaking as a horrible, screaming laugh from somewhere in the jungle reached their ears.

"What's that?" Bess queried.

"A hyena," the White Hunter replied.

He and his wife looked at each other. Nancy was sure they were wondering how Swahili Joe had fared. Had some wild beast got the man's scent and come for him?

Although Nancy disliked Swahili Joe intensely, the thought of such a horrible death for him made her shiver. Then, thinking of what he had been guilty of, she began to reflect who was more cruel and cunning—the wild animals or man?

Ned interrupted her train of thought and said, "Let's go watch the elephants some more. I want to take a few more pictures."

They returned to the porch and watched. It seemed to the young people as if the elephants would never get enough water to drink. They moved around very little and only once in a while did they trumpet. This happened when one of them was annoyed by another elephant.

Although Nancy enjoyed the mystical scene in front of her, lighted only by the dim yellow glow of subdued searchlights, her mind kept reverting to the spider sapphire mystery. Here she was in the middle of the jungle and yet the mystery had pursued her on two occasions. First she had been told by one of the Indian guests that he believed there was a fraud in connection with the reported theft of the gem. Then the man believed to be Swahili Joe had suddenly appeared.

"It's all very weird," she thought.

The following morning Nancy and the rest of the Emerson group were up early. At breakfast they recounted the various activities of the animals which they had seen. Nancy hardly took part in the conversation. Her mind was still on the mystery. Now she was going back to Nairobi to hear the strange story of Tizam's disappearance.

That afternoon Nancy and her friends went to have tea with Mrs. Munger. Their hostess proved to be a charming woman who was very well informed on the subjects of African history and jungle lore.

After tea had been served, she began her story. The guide Tizam had been an unusually intelligent and helpful one. Her safari had reached a rest camp and Tizam had gone off by himself.

"Unfortunately he never returned," Mrs. Munger said. "We felt very sad about it. After we waited a couple of days for him, we interviewed some other guides and then moved on with one of them, named Butubu."

The new guide had told of seeing a native defending himself against a lioness. From a description of him, she was sure he was Tizam.

Butubu had screamed and beat on trees to distract the beast's attention. This had given him a chance to throw his spear and kill the lioness.

"Butubu himself was nearly set upon by another lioness, so he ran off to safety. Later he and his friends returned to the spot. The man was not there and they found no trace of him. Apparently he had not been killed because there was no evidence of this."

"How amazing!" said Nancy. "Then where did he go?"

Mrs. Munger replied, "Perhaps he was found by members of some tribe and taken to their village to be cared for."

"But he'd be well by this time and could have returned," Nancy said.

"That's true," Mrs. Munger agreed. "That is part of the great mystery surrounding Tizam."

CHAPTER XII

Surprise Meeting

"THEN there is a good chance that the guide Tizam is alive," said Nancy. She was excited at the thought of how happy Madame Lilia Bulawaya would be if Nancy succeeded in locating him.

"I hope he is alive," Munger replied. "He's a very nice man and I understand talented. I did not find out what it is he does. Acting as a guide was just a sideline."

When tea was over and the young guests were saying good-by to their hostess, she asked where they were going next.

"To the Mount Kenya Safari Club early tomorrow morning," Nancy told her.

"That is a beautiful spot," Mrs. Munger remarked. "With magnificent snow-capped Mount Kenya in the distance and the grounds— Well, you'll see for yourself."

The Safari Club and the surrounding country were as beautiful as Mrs. Munger had said. The extensive grounds were attractively laid out, with beautiful gardens and inviting play areas. At the foot of a grassy slope was a series of ponds. One was a swimming pool for guests; the other ponds were homes for various kinds of birds. Crested cranes stalked about the lawns. Swans, both white and rare black ones, swam serenely among water lilies on one of the ponds.

"It's heavenly here!" Bess remarked. She was admiring the view from the girls' first-floor bedroom window.

The room was large and had three beds in it. Living-room furniture, attractive drapes, and a fireplace at one end gave the place a cozy atmosphere.

There was a knock on the door and a smiling black boy entered, his arms full of logs. With a pleasant "Good morning," he knelt down and built a fire. Because of a slight chill in the air, the girls were delighted to have the fire. The boy bowed and went out.

"Since we're going to be here a little while," Bess spoke up, "I'm going to hang up my dresses. They really can stand an airing."

The girls hung up their suits and dresses. They left the rest of their clothes and jewelry in the suitcases.

"It would be fun to have our breakfast in front of this fire," George remarked, "but we promised to meet the boys, so we'd better go."

"Actually this is our second breakfast," Nancy reminded the others. "But I must admit I can use it after that drive up here."

As usual, Bess said, "I'm starved!"

While the girls were walking through the attractive club to the dining room, Bess remarked, "This looks like a safe place for us to be. No villains, baboons, or anything else to bother us. We can just have fun and forget all the mysteries."

Nancy made no comment, but she thought that surely her enemies knew the Emerson itinerary. It was doubtful they would leave her and her friends alone.

"I just hope I'll see them first," Nancy said to herself.

The breakfast hour was jolly and at the end Nancy suggested that they all put on bathing suits and go to the swimming pool.

"Great idea," Burt agreed.

"And I can do some sun-tanning," said George.

Bess warned her cousin to be careful of the strong African sun. "I hear it will give you a terrible burn without you realizing you're turning to a crisp."

When the young people left the dining room,

Ned and Nancy were last in line. As they strolled through the lobby, Nancy whispered to him, "See that Indian over there in the corner reading a newspaper."

Ned looked in the direction which she indicated. The man was elderly. He was handsome with his shock of white hair and wore his English-style clothes well.

"That's some ring he's wearing," Ned remarked.

On the little finger of the Indian's left hand was a ring with a large flashing diamond.

Nancy was more interested in a name penciled in an upper corner of the newspaper. "Ned, it says Tagore! Do you suppose he's Shastri Tagore?"

"Maybe."

"Let's ask the desk clerk," she suggested.

"Why don't we just introduce ourselves?" Ned proposed.

Nancy was tempted to follow his suggestion, but on second thought changed her mind. "If it is Mr. Tagore, why don't I ask when he made his reservation? It's just possible he came here because of us."

Ned agreed and went with her to the desk. To the couple's surprise, they learned that indeed the man was Mr. Shastri Tagore from Mombasa and that he came here year after year at exactly this time.

The clerk seemed somewhat amused at Nancy and Ned's interest in the man. "Would you like to meet him?" he asked.

Nancy blushed but said, "Yes, I would."

The clerk escorted the couple to where Mr. Tagore was reading. As soon as introductions were made, he excused himself and returned to his desk.

Mr. Tagore had risen and it was evident at once that he was a very polite and cultured man. "You are from the United States? How interesting! Won't you sit down? I should like to ask you some questions about your country."

For several minutes the conversation remained general. Every subject which was touched upon was one with which Mr. Tagore seemed very familiar, even sports in America. He talked with Ned for several minutes about football and then with Nancy about tennis.

"Do you ride?" Mr. Tagore asked them. When both nodded, he said, "If you are ever in Mombasa, I wish you would come to see me. I have horses which I believe you would enjoy riding."

All this time Nancy was thinking, "How could this fine-appearing gentleman possibly be part of a jewel fraud?" It was some time before it seemed opportune to mention the subject uppermost in her mind but finally the opportunity came. "I understand that you own a fabulous spider sapphire which disappeared."

"Yes. It was stolen, I am afraid." Then a puzzled frown crossed his forehead. "But you are from the States. How did you know about this?"

"Because I'm from River Heights," she answered.

At this, Mr. Tagore looked blank and said, "I do not understand."

Nancy felt sure that if he did know about Mr. Ramsey's synthetic gem, he would not have placed much value on it. She was not ready yet, however, to give up trying to find out all she could from him.

Nancy asked, "How would one tell a real spider sapphire from a modern synthetic one?"

The Indian smiled. "I greatly doubt that anyone could fashion such a gem, but if he were clever enough to do so, there would be a sure way to tell the difference."

Nancy and Ned waited for Mr. Tagore to continue. Here was a marvelous clue! If he chose to tell them—

Mr. Tagore went on, "Millions of years ago the spiders on this earth had no spinnerets. The one in my sapphire has none."

"How amazing!" Nancy remarked.

She was tempted to tell Mr. Tagore about the Ramsey synthetic gem. No doubt the modern spider in it did have spinnerets. But she decided to find out more about this man before revealing what she knew. Nancy asked him why the ancient spiders apparently did not need to spin threads and weave webs to trap their food.

"The original spiders lived on the water," Mr. Tagore replied. "Later, when some of them became land arachnids, they developed spinnerets." He paused for a moment and looked quizzically at Nancy. "I have a feeling, Miss Drew, that there is something of greater interest to you on this subject than the history of spiders."

Nancy smiled and said, "I heard a rumor that your stolen gem is in the United States."

Mr. Tagore looked surprised and shook his head. "That is not the truth," he said. "It is still somewhere in Africa."

Ned asked, "Where do you think it went?"

The Indian looked around, making sure that no one could hear him. He whispered, "I believe it was taken by a guide who later disappeared."

"A guide?" Nancy repeated. "You mean a guide on a safari?"

"Exactly. The guide was reported to be looking for a relative of his who was captured by a raiding tribe in the jungle."

"But you do not believe this story?" Ned queried.

Mr. Tagore thought a moment. "I do not know what to believe. So many theories have come to me that I am utterly confused. But this story about the guide seemed the most likely. I think he is in hiding."

"What were the names of the guide and the relative he was looking for?" Nancy asked.

"Chotu was the relative—and let me think. Oh yes, the guide's name was Tizam."

CHAPTER XIII

A Disastrous Fire

TIZAM was suspected of being one of the thieves involved in the stolen spider sapphire mystery! Nancy and Ned could not help but show surprise.

Mr. Tagore looked at them puzzled and asked, "You know these men?"

"Not Chotu," Nancy replied. "But we have heard of Tizam. He has a sister who is a singer. She's in America. When she learned we were coming to Africa, she mentioned her brother."

"Did she tell you that he was reported to have disappeared?" the Indian asked.

Nancy felt that she should reveal no more and merely said, "She mentioned something of the sort. Have you any idea where he is?"

"No," said Mr. Tagore. "If I had, I would send the authorities after him."

Nancy's mind was in a whirl. What a strange combination of stories there were about Tizam's trek into the jungle! He was reported to have been mauled and killed by a lioness. He was supposed to have been rescued but disappeared. Now he was being accused of theft and staying in hiding!

Nancy said to Mr. Tagore, "I certainly hope that the person or persons who took your spider sapphire will be found."

The couple said good-by and went off. They continued to discuss the strange turn of events, but presently Ned asked, "What's next on our program, Nancy?"

"We're all to meet at the swimming pool," Nancy reminded him.

"Then I'll see you in a few minutes," Ned said, and hurried off toward his room.

By the time Nancy had reached hers, Bess and George were already in their suits. Nancy quickly changed and the three girls went outside. The day was sunny and very warm.

"How beautiful Mount Kenya is!" Bess exclaimed, looking into the distance. "Just think! Snow all year round near the equator!"

Tables with umbrellas were set up around the pool. Gwen, looking extremely attractive, came over with Hal to join the girls.

"Water's wonderful!" she said.

Hal remarked, "Gwen's a real nymph." She blushed, but it was evident she enjoyed the compliment.

In a few minutes Ned, Burt, and Dave joined the group. There was a lively exchange of teasing and witty wisecracks.

Presently Ned said, "Fellows, how about a race to the end of the pool and back?"

"Sure thing," Burt responded and took his place at the edge. Dave swung into position alongside him, Hal next, and Ned fourth.

George was elected to call out the start and to be the judge of the winner. She stood behind the boys and said:

"Ready! Get set! Go!"

The four swimmers dived in. Each one made a long underwater swim. When he rose to the surface, the racer plowed madly along to the opposite end of the pool, gave a quick push with one foot, and started back. Each of the four girls egged on her particular friend.

"Go!"

"Hurry up!"

"Swim, swim!"

"Give it to 'em!" George cried out, rooting for Burt, although she was supposed to be an impartial judge.

Whether it was her cry of encouragement, or because Burt was the best swimmer, no one could say, but he did come in first and was pronounced the winner.

As he climbed from the water, shaking his head to get the water off, he said with a grin, "I like

Africa! This is the first race I've won in a long time!"

By now most of the others in the Emerson safari had gathered and soon the pool was full of swimmers. There was some horseplay, then finally everyone came to sit in the chairs or on towels spread on the ground. One of the boys had brought a transistor radio. When he turned it on, they could hear an American record being played.

"That music makes it seem as if we weren't so far away from home," Bess spoke up.

Record after record of American-composed songs and dances followed. Presently a waltz came on.

Ned stood up and called out, "How about you girls putting on a show? A water ballet?"

"Good idea," said Gwen. "Come on, girls!"

Without time for any rehearsing, the performers were forced to make up their own ballet. From the enthusiastic clapping, they judged it was good. It was evident to the watching boys, however, that Gwen Taylor far outshone the others. She was grace personified in the water and Hal's remark about her being a nymph was true.

As the record ended and the girls pulled themselves up over the side of the pool, the boys clapped loudly. Then Ned said, "We didn't call this a contest and we have no prize, but I'd like to tell you, Gwen, that you're a beautiful dancing swimmer."

"Oh, thank you, but I thought everybody else was marvelous," she said.

Some in the group who were not yet aware of Gwen's change of attitude looked at her in amazement. Many of them crowded around her and she knew from this that she was now "in."

Someone called out, "It's almost lunchtime. Meet you all on the patio." The meal was to be served here.

The swimmers arose and walked toward the club. Nancy, Bess, and George, towels around their shoulders, went up the slight incline of the beautiful green lawn and entered the main building. They got the key to their room from the desk clerk.

As Nancy unlocked their door, Bess remarked, "Phew! What a horrible odor!"

The three girls walked through the short hallway and stepped inside the room. They looked around. Suddenly all of them gave a gasp of dismay.

Heaped in the fireplace were the remains of their burned clothing and suitcases!

The girls rushed forward disbelievingly. In a moment Bess burst into tears. "My lovely dresses!" she wailed.

George's face turned red with anger. She went to the closet and opened it. Every dress was gone.

"This is an outrage!" she stormed.

Nancy was grim. For several moments she said

Heaped in the fireplace were their burned clothing and suitcases

nothing. What vandal had been in here and done such a sadistic thing? "Our enemies!" she decided.

Turning on her heel, Nancy went out the door and hurried to the manager's office. She told him what had happened and asked him to come and see the damage. Upon looking at the still smoldering fire, he stood still in amazement.

Then he turned to the girls. "Why would anyone do such a thing? I'll get the room boy at once and see if he knows anything about this."

He telephoned to the employees' quarters and in minutes the room boy arrived.

"Roscoe, do you know anything about this?" he asked.

When the boy saw the mess in the fireplace he stared at it blankly, and denied any knowledge of the vandalism. Roscoe said he had brought in more wood, tidied up the room, then gone out and locked the door.

"Someone must have come in through the open window," Nancy said to the manager.

He excused the room boy, who went off. "I'm sure Roscoe is honest," he said. "And anyway, what would he have to gain by burning your belongings?"

The girls agreed. Finally Nancy told the manager that she was trying to solve a mystery here in Africa.

"I think that certain people who don't want me to learn the facts perpetrated this outrage."

The thought went through her mind, "Could it possibly have been Mr. Tagore?" It seemed unlikely, yet from the beginning she had wondered if he might be involved in the theft.

The manager offered to send someone to town immediately to purchase clothes for the girls. "Thank you," said Nancy, "but I think we can borrow enough from our friends to last us until we get to Nairobi."

Bess spoke up. "Let's ask Gwen first. She has lots of clothes."

The manager and Bess left together. She returned in a few minutes saying that Gwen was delighted and would herself take charge of asking for donations from the other girls. Within fifteen minutes she knocked on their door and came in with her arms loaded. Behind her were two other girls, one of them carrying a suitcase which contained underwear and shoes.

"Oh my goodness!" said George. "I couldn't wear all these clothes in a week!"

"This is like Christmas," Bess added. She had spotted a frilly white dress and said, "Nancy and George, do you mind if I take this one?"

"No," Nancy replied. "It looks just like you."

The various articles of clothing were distributed. As the three from River Heights gazed at themselves in the mirror a few minutes later, George grinned and said:

"Who am I?"

Gwen giggled. "I think you're Dot Bird. Nancy, you look lovely in the light-blue linen that used to be mine."

By the time the River Heights girls reached the patio, the story of the fire in their room had spread among other guests. Mr. Tagore left his table and came over to speak to Nancy. She introduced her friends.

"I am sorry to hear about your loss," he said. "Only someone with a criminal mind could have done such a thing. I regret that Africa has treated you so badly."

"It was a great loss indeed," Nancy answered. "But our friends kindly shared their clothes with us."

Mr. Tagore asked whether the three girls had also lost the jewelry they had brought.

"Yes, we did," Bess replied. "It was in the suitcases and the fire ruined everything."

"Perhaps," Mr. Tagore suggested, "the jewelry was not burned but was stolen."

Nancy had not thought of this possibility and agreed that it could be true.

Mr. Tagore had evidently finished his lunch because he said good-by and went into the hotel.

Nancy and her friends found two tables under a flame tree overlooking the large grassy area, which was surrounded by other small, tree-shaded tables. To one side were spits on which turkeys, squabs, and pigs were roasting. In front of these stood long tables loaded with a variety of food, including tropical fruits. Smiling chefs were in attendance to help serve the buffet.

Bess was ecstatic and started to heap her plate. One dark glance from George and she put back a luscious-looking pork chop.

Halfway through the meal, Ned said, "Here come the dancers."

Members of the Choku tribe, all men, appeared from a rear garden. Their gay costumes included short, fringed skirts, large shaggy headdresses, and anklets. They carried bongo drums between their knees and moved in a circle as they played and danced. Each motion was part of a story. At times the men swung the drums under one arm. Every so often they would squat.

"The rhythm is great," said Dave. "And the dance is not very different from some of ours. Now at our next fraternity dance maybe I'll get a costume, a bongo drum, and—"

"Dave Evans," said Bess, "if you dare show up in a brief costume like these men are wearing, I—I won't let on I know you!"

An hour later the group left the patio. The plan was to take a hike and later go swimming. Nancy, Bess, and George decided to change their clothes and went to the desk for their room key.

The clerk handed each girl a gift-wrapped package. Smiling, he said, "These are with Mr. Tagore's compliments."

CHAPTER XIV

Into Lion Country

PUZZLED and amazed by the gifts from Mr. Tagore, Nancy, Bess, and George hurried to their room and tore off the wrappings. In each box lay a necklace of African semiprecious stones.

"They're beautiful!" Bess exclaimed. "I guess Mr. Tagore's pretty nice after all."

George, who rarely wore jewelry, clasped her necklace around her neck and looked in the mirror. "Hm! This will go well with sports clothes."

Nancy was very pleased with her necklace. It was a little more elaborate than that of the other girls and had bold beads between African jade stones. She had seen it in the window of one of the club's shops.

Suddenly George turned around and said, "As long as we suspect Mr. Tagore of being implicated in the spider sapphire disappearance, I think we should return these gifts."

"Oh no!" Bess cried. "I don't believe he's a crook. He has a real nice face. I don't care what you do, but I'm going to keep my necklace."

Nancy smiled. "Whatever we do, let's not be hasty. Even if Mr. Tagore sent this gift to throw us off the scent, we ought to have a little more proof that he's not an honest man."

"How do you hope to do that?" George asked.

"By making a few discreet inquiries among the hotel personnel," Nancy answered. "I'll begin at the desk."

Bess pleaded that she not start her investigation now. The girls had promised to meet their friends at the pool. "Once you get to sleuthing, no telling how long it will take. Ned will be furious."

Nancy laughed and agreed to wait until after the swim period was over.

It was close to six o'clock before the girls returned to their rooms. Nancy dressed at once, this time in an intriguing print of African animals donated by a girl named Beth Jones. The young detective walked out to the desk and began talking to the desk clerk about the hotel's evening entertainment. Gradually she turned the conversation to Mr. Tagore.

The clerk said, "He's a very fine gentleman. Been coming to the club for six years. He's a great lover of birds and enjoys our collection very much."

"And he's very fond of jewelry too, I assume,"

Nancy said. "He wore a beautiful diamond ring and gave us three girls necklaces."

"That's just like him," the clerk said. "Always doing thoughtful things for other people."

At that moment an arriving guest took the clerk's attention and Nancy went to her room. She reported the clerk's high opinion of Mr. Tagore.

"That settles it," said Bess. "If we try to return these necklaces now, we'd only hurt his feelings. I think all we should do is thank him."

The other two agreed. But when they looked for Mr. Tagore in the dining room, he was not in sight. Finally the girls wandered back to the desk and asked the clerk where he thought they might locate him.

"Mr. Tagore has checked out," the man said. "He left here about two hours ago."

"For Mombasa?" Nancy asked.

"Yes."

The girls turned away and Bess said, "I guess we'll have to call on Mr. Tagore in Mombasa to thank him."

Two mornings later the Emerson group left the Safari Club. There was not a single clue to the person who had burned the suitcases and clothes of Nancy and her roommates. After checking in at their Nairobi hotel, the three girls went shopping. First they bought suitcases, then went from shop to shop filling them.

Everything proved to be easy to find except

shoes. They bought some for rough walking but saw nothing for dressy wear except styles with extremely high, narrow heels. They did not want these.

"I guess we'll have to keep wearing the borrowed ones," George said finally. "I'm tired of shopping. Let's go home!"

They took a taxi back to the hotel. At once they changed to some newly purchased attire, and called the laundry service for a quick cleaning job before returning the borrowed apparel.

At that moment Gwen wandered into the room. When she heard the plan, she refused to take back anything she had given and said the other girls in the group felt the same way.

Nancy laughed. "You're all wonderful. Anyway, if you want to borrow any of your own clothes, let us know!"

Nancy telephoned Ned and asked if he would accompany her to the agency for which Tizam had worked.

"Meet you in five minutes," Ned replied.

The agency was within walking distance of the hotel. When Nancy and Ned entered the office, the staff was busy with clients who were planning safaris. Nancy noticed that one of the men was free, so she and Ned approached him.

"Won't you both sit down?" he said. "I'm Mr. Foster."

As they seated themselves, Nancy said, "We'd

like to get some information about a guide you used to have named Tizam."

Mr. Foster heaved a sigh. "I wish I could give you some definite information but really I have none."

Nancy looked disappointed. Mr. Foster went on, "Since you are asking about Tizam, I suppose you know he was lost on a safari. Rumor has it that he was mauled by a lioness."

Nancy told him of the other theory that Tizam might still be alive. "I understand another man saw him being attacked, but killed the lioness before she had mauled Tizam to death."

Mr. Foster nodded. "Yes, there was that story, but we at this office thought it was probably exaggerated."

Ned asked Mr. Foster what kind of man Tizam was. There was an immediate enthusiastic answer. "A very fine guide and a most trustworthy man. Everyone spoke highly of him."

After a pause, Nancy asked, "He wouldn't be the kind of person to steal any jewels?"

"Oh no," Mr. Foster answered. "He was a very upright young man. His loss to us has been great. We have never found anyone to replace him."

Nancy told Mr. Foster about having met Madame Lilia Bulawaya and of Nancy's promise to try locating her brother Tizam. "Have you any suggestions as to how I might go about this?"

Mr. Foster looked into space for several seconds.

Then he said, "I could arrange a safari for you."

"Would it be very expensive and how long would it take?" Nancy queried.

Mr. Foster smiled. "Since your errand has to do with Tizam I would give you a special rate. You could go by Land Rover to the spot where he was attacked and be back in one day. I could supply a driver."

"Ned, do you think we should do it?" Nancy asked. "I'm sure the Stanleys would agree if all our crowd could go."

Reluctantly Ned reminded her that they were to fly the next morning to Mombasa. To change the schedule would upset sightseeing plans for everyone.

Nancy sighed, but already a plan was formulating in her mind. She would ask Professor and Mrs. Stanley if her group of six might stay over one day in order to make the trip.

She mentioned this aloud to Mr. Foster. "If I obtain their permission, could you get the Land Rover for tomorrow?"

"Yes, and I could arrange for Butubu to go with you, if you like."

"That would be perfect." Nancy was thrilled. "Ned, let's hurry back to the hotel and find the Stanleys."

First Nancy and Ned approached Burt and Dave and then Bess and George to see if they wanted to make the somewhat dangerous trip.

"I'll go," Bess said, "but I certainly hope we don't meet any lions."

Professor and Mrs. Stanley did not give permission at once, but a little later decided that Nancy and her friends could be relied upon to take care of themselves. With promises of acting with extreme caution, the young people thanked their chaperons.

Early the next morning a large black-and-white-striped Land Rover came to the hotel. The driver introduced himself as Butubu. He had a good-natured smile and was very pleasant. In addition to this, Nancy knew from what she had heard about him that he was fearless and brave in the jungle.

The Land Rover zipped along at a good pace, and though the road was rough, its passengers made no complaints. After a while Butubu announced that he was going to stop at the hippo pool.

"There are two good things to take pictures of," he said. "Have your cameras ready."

He stopped the bus and walked forward to where two blacks stood in uniform. The men spoke to one another in Swahili.

The Americans noticed the unusual ear lobes of one of the men. There was a large hole in the center of each one and the flesh hung down in a long loop. Attached were earrings that almost touched the man's shoulder. Bess snapped their picture. The two guides led the way through woodland to a large pool at the foot of a grassy, stubbly hillside.

"Watch carefully and you may see a hippo come out of the water," Butubu said. "By the way, these guides belong to the Masai tribe. Formerly it was a custom to treat the ears this way, probably as a tribal identification."

"I don't see any hippos," Bess complained.

She was holding her camera ready to shoot at an instant's notice. Bess turned to Butubu.

"Would you mind standing alongside these guides and I'll snap all three of you?"

The men lined up. Bess looked into the finder and decided she should stand a little farther back. Inadvertently she stepped too far back and the next moment lost her balance. She began rolling down the hillside!

In an instant Dave went after her. It was evident from his long strides that he would soon overtake Bess.

But the camera had flown out of Bess's hands. Now it was bouncing downhill. Nancy rushed after it, but the chase seemed hopeless. In another few seconds the camera would drop into the water!

With a final sprint Nancy reached the camera just in time. At the same instant she saw a huge hippo rising out of the water almost directly in front of her. Quickly adjusting the camera she snapped a picture. Then she climbed the hillside.

As Nancy handed the camera to Bess, she said, "I hope this wasn't broken and I got a good shot for you."

Bess examined the camera and it seemed to be all right. "Thanks a million," she said. "I never would have made that good shot myself."

The young people and their guides walked back to the bus and climbed in. No more stops were made. Soon Butubu turned into an area which had no visible road, merely very tall grass and here and there some trees.

Wary of lions, Butubu ordered the group to stay in the Land Rover. Slowly he wound his way along, then finally drew to a halt.

He pointed ahead to the shelter of some trees. "Over there is where I saw Tizam and the lioness," he said.

At that moment six blacks rose up from the tall grass. They held spears ready to throw and advanced toward the Land Rover.

CHAPTER XV

Native's Help

In an instant the whole Emerson group dropped to the floor of the bus. Would the native warriors try to break in upon them?

"This is terrible!" came Bess's muffled wail.

The Americans could hear Butubu calling out in Swahili to the oncoming men. There was a long conversation, which did not sound hostile to Nancy. In fact, she heard a couple of the spearmen laugh.

Cautiously she raised her head and looked out the window. The tribesmen stood with their spears pointed toward the ground and did not appear at all menacing now. Finally Nancy stood up and spoke to Butubu.

"Everything is all right," he said. "No danger."

Somewhat sheepishly the young people got up from the floor and took their seats. Butubu explained that these men were stalking a roving lioness. She was reported to have killed a child in one of the villages.

"How horrible!" Bess exclaimed.

Butubu nodded. "These men were amused that you thought they meant to harm you."

"It wasn't so funny," Bess complained.

Nancy asked the guide to find out if the natives knew or had heard of Tizam. He questioned the men, then translated the answer.

"A year ago a man dragged himself into their tribe's village. He had been mauled by a lioness but had survived the attack."

"Did they find out who he was?" George asked.

Butubu shook his head. "The man had lost his memory. He had developed fever and it took a long time for the medicine man to make him well. After a while his body was all right, but he could not remember who he was or where he came from."

"Is he still at their village?" Nancy queried.

Butubu questioned the natives, but the answer was No. The stranger had disappeared one night and they had no idea where he had gone.

Nancy and her friends were dismayed and alarmed to hear this. If the man was Tizam, there was no telling where he might have wandered. He might even have lost his life. In any case, it would account for his never having communicated with his sister or Mr. Foster's agency.

George said in disappointment, "Just when we were getting within reach of solving the mystery, it slips right through our fingers!"

Nancy continued to ask questions, hoping to elicit some clue to Tizam's whereabouts. She learned that several times, in somewhat lucid moments, Tizam had said in Swahili, "I must get to Mombasa and report those thieves to the police."

"What do you think he meant?" Dave queried. "Something to do with the spider sapphire?"

Nancy requested Butubu to ask the tribesmen if Tizam had carried any gems with him.

"No, he had nothing in his pockets and no identification."

Burt spoke up. "I doubt that we can learn any more. Don't you think we should start back for Nairobi?"

Butubu nodded, but when he told this to the spearmen, they objected. The guide translated that the men insisted the visitors come to their village for a meal and a ceremonial dance.

"I am afraid you cannot deny them this pleasure," Butubu said.

The natives started their trek to the village and the bus followed slowly. No one saw any lions, but Butubu pointed out graceful elands and kudus. They resembled American deer but their horns were quite different. Those of the elands were long and straight and pointed slightly backwards.

The kudus' rose straight up from the forehead and curved in such a way that from a distance they resembled snakes.

Suddenly Butubu stopped the bus. "Look!" he said, pointing toward a tree-shaded area. "There's a family of hyrax. In Africa we call them dassies."

"Aren't they cute?" Bess exclaimed. "Are they some kind of rabbit?"

"No," Butubu replied. "If you will look closely, you will see that they have no tails. People used to think they belonged to the rat family. But scientists made a study of their bodies and say their nearest relatives are the elephants."

"Hard to believe," said Burt. "Think of a rabbit-sized elephant!"

The small, dark-brown animals were sunning themselves on an outcropping of rocks. Three babies were hopping about their mother. Butubu explained that they were among the most interesting African animals.

"The babies start walking around within a few minutes of their birth and after the first day they're on their own. They return to the mother only long enough to be fed, but they start eating greens very quickly."

Butubu drove on but continued to talk about the dassies. "There is an amusing folk tale about these little animals. It was said that in the days when the earth was first formed and animals were being put on it, the weather was cold and rainy.

"When all the animals were called to a certain spot to be given tails, the dassie did not want to go. As other kinds passed him, he begged them to bring him back a tail."

Nancy laughed. "But none of them did."

"That is right," Butubu answered. "And so to this day they have no tails that they can use to switch flies."

Everyone in the bus thanked him for relating the charming little legend, then looked out the windows. They were approaching a village of grass-roofed huts. The small homes were built in a semicircle.

The spearmen called out to some of the villagers and men of all ages and women and children came running from the huts. When the visitors were announced, some of the natives hastened back inside.

"They are putting on their ceremonial dress," Butubu said.

The visitors got out of the bus and were asked to sit on the ground. The meal would soon be served to them. It was not long in arriving and consisted of wildebeest stew and mealies, a sort of coarse cornmeal mush.

Bess looked askance as her bowl was heaped with the steaming stew and the mealies put on top of it. Nancy and George were amused by the expression on her face. For once Bess was not saying, "This looks delicious!"

Nancy was the first one to dip her crude wooden spoon into the food. She announced that it was delicious, although salt-free and rather flat. Everyone was hungry and soon all the bowls were empty. The handsome native children smiled shyly as they served wild grapes for dessert. The fruit was sweet and tasty.

In a few moments several men appeared, drums hanging from their shoulders. They stood in front of the guests, then began swaying left and right as they beat on the instruments. There were several different songs. With some, the men moved forward and backward; with others, they remained in a kneeling posture.

Presently they laid their drums on the ground. They sat down, and beat upon them softly as they began to sing the next song.

Startled, Nancy sat upright. It was the tune she had learned from Madame Lilia Bulawaya! Unconsciously she began to hum it, then sang the words with the men.

When the dance was over, the men stood up. A tribesman, whom Butubu said was the chief, came over to Nancy. He said something to her in Swahili, which Butubu translated.

"We are charmed that you know our song. Please stand up with the dancers and sing it."

Nancy blushed a deep red. "Oh, I couldn't. I don't know it that well," she protested.

The natives would not take No for an answer.

The chief took her hand and raised Nancy from the ground, then escorted her forward to the dancing group.

To herself Nancy was saying, "Oh, I hope I don't muff this! I suppose it is the least I can do in return for the meal."

The drums began to beat softly and the men hummed just above a whisper. This was Nancy's cue. Raising her voice, she sang the lovely lullaby just as Madame Bulawaya had taught her.

At the end the natives were enthusiastic. They beat on the drums, stamped on the ground, and shouted their applause. Nancy bowed several times, then sat down with her friends.

"That was great!" Ned praised her. "I expect they will make you a princess of this tribe."

Nancy's eyes twinkled. "And have me become one of the chief's wives?" Then she became serious. She knew that while tribal customs were kept, the men, women and children were becoming more civilized and educated all the time and polygamy was fast becoming a thing of the past.

When the entertainment was over, Nancy and her friends stood up and asked Butubu to thank the chief for the friendly hospitality and to tell him it was an experience they would never forget. The leader grinned broadly and hoped they would all come again—they would always be most welcome.

The visitors returned to the bus and drove back

to Nairobi. They discussed the new clue to Tizam and asked Nancy what she intended to do next to solve the mystery about him.

"It's only a hunch, but I have a strong feeling that he's still alive and I'm going to work harder than ever to find him."

"In Mombasa?" Ned asked.

"Probably. Now I can hardly wait to get there."

She and her friends reached the hotel in time for a very late dinner. As she stopped at the desk to get her key, the clerk said that two men, one older than the other, had called on her that morning.

"They wouldn't leave their names, but said they were most eager to get in touch with you," he reported.

"What time were they here?" Nancy asked.

The clerk said he did not remember exactly, but that it was before the rest of the Emerson group had left for Mombasa. "The men seemed very annoyed to learn that you were not here."

Nancy asked for a description of the two men. It was possible they were Jahan and Dhan! From what little the clerk could remember, however, it was hard to tell.

"One of the men mumbled something about having to wait all day for you to return," the clerk said. "Oh, I forgot to mention that they'll be back this evening."

Deep in thought Nancy walked to the elevator,

where her friends were waiting for her. On the way upstairs she told them what she had just learned.

"I don't like this," Ned commented. "Nancy, please don't see those men alone. I'll stick around and make sure that you're safe!"

"And I'll certainly be glad to have you." Nancy smiled.

It was decided they would not spend much time dressing, as everyone was hungry. Besides, the dining room would soon close. They hurried and met downstairs. The young people had just finished dinner when one of the hotel boys handed Nancy a small silver platter. On it lay a note signed by the desk clerk. It read:

"Messrs. Brown and Ross who came earlier today to see you are waiting in the lobby."

As Nancy rose from the table, her heart began to beat a little faster at the thought of what might lie ahead of her.

CHAPTER XVI

Swahili Joe

NANCY and Ned hurried into the lobby. The clerk nodded toward two men near the door. They were not Jahan and Dhan, but they definitely were Indians.

"Miss Drew?" one of them said. "I'm Mr. Brown. This is Mr. Ross."

Nancy introduced Ned Nickerson but the Indians did not put out their hands to shake Ned's. She quickly sized up the two callers. Her intuition warned her that these men had hard, cruel characters.

"Miss Drew," said Brown, "we understand that you have a great interest in Mr. Tagore's spider sapphire."

"An interest?" Nancy replied. "I have heard it is very beautiful and I think it's too bad that the gem is missing."

"Indeed it is," Mr. Ross agreed. "We would

like your honest opinion about the gem we read about on display in the River Heights Museum."

Both Nancy and Ned were thinking the same thing: Why would these men be interested in a synthetic gem fashioned so many thousands of miles away, unless they were somehow connected with the loss of Mr. Tagore's property?

"There is little I can tell you," Nancy said. "My father personally knows the man who created the gem in the museum. It is synthetic. I have been told that Mr. Tagore's gem was formed by nature millions of years ago."

There was a slight lull in the conversation while Brown and Ross seemed to be trying to decide what to say next.

Ned broke the silence. "How did you men learn about Mr. Ramsey's gem?"

Ross answered, "From the newspaper."

"But what is your interest in it?"

Ross's eyes snapped. "What's yours?"

Ned did not reply. Instead he turned to Nancy and said, "Come on! Let's go!"

Nancy hesitated. Looking directly at the two Indians, who, she felt sure, were using assumed names, she asked, "Where is Swahili Joe now?"

Ross was taken off guard. Before realizing it, he replied, "In Mom—" Then he stopped short.

A frightened look came over Mr. Brown's face. Tugging at Ross's sleeve, he urged him to leave. The two men dashed from the hotel.

For a second Nancy and Ned stood looking after them. Then suddenly Ned turned and hurried toward Bess, George, Burt, and Dave, who had just reached the lobby. He said excitedly, "Come on, fellows!"

"What's up?" Burt queried.

"Tell you later," Ned replied, and ran from the hotel. The other two boys were right behind him.

Nancy knew what Ned had in mind. He wanted to overtake Brown and Ross and find out the real reason for their coming to see Nancy. The thought worried the young detective and she called out: '

"Don't go!"

But Ned and his fraternity brothers paid no attention. Soon they were out of sight.

The boys spotted Brown and Ross running down a side street. The men sped down the next block and turned into a business section where the shops now were closed. There were neither pedestrians nor traffic at the moment.

In a few minutes the three boys overtook the men. "Stop!" Ned called out.

Brown and Ross did as he suggested. But before Ned could speak to them, the men lashed out at the three boys. The Indians' muscles seemed to be made of steel.

Burt received a punch on the forehead which made him see stars, but it angered him so much he retaliated like a prize fighter. Dave was punched in the stomach and he doubled up with pain. Ned was trying to tackle both opponents at once.

The tide of battle became one-sided when reinforcements arrived for Ross and Brown. Two more men joined the melee with fists flying.

One of them was a black and powerful. Ned just had time to cry out, "Swahili Joe!" when the man caught him with a swift uppercut to the jaw that knocked him unconscious.

The tussle continued, but Burt and Dave were fast losing ground. Then Brown, Ross, and one of the others suddenly sped off. Burt and Dave were puzzled until they turned and looked the other way. Approaching on a run were four policemen!

Swahili Joe saw them too. In a swift move he picked Ned up and swung him across one shoulder, then leaped down the street.

Burt and Dave, though almost exhausted, ran after the big fellow and yanked Ned from him. Swahili Joe did not protest. He took to his heels and was out of sight before the police arrived.

The four officers asked what had happened. Quickly Burt explained.

"I see you do not need us," one of the men said. "Your attackers have gone. Did they get anything?"

Dave answered. "Those men aren't ordinary thugs. They didn't try to rob us. But our friend here was kidnapped and the big man was the guard."

At that moment Ned sat up, shook his head, and said, "He sure was—back in the States."

This announcement surprised the policemen, who said they would try to find him. "What is the man's name?" one of the officers asked.

Ned answered, "His nickname is Swahili Joe. We think he's connected with the thieves who stole the spider sapphire."

Burt took up the story. "Those men who ran away first are also part of the ring, we think."

The leader of the police team said that one man would accompany the boys back to the hotel to be sure they were all right and would not be attacked again. The other three would start an immediate search for the assailants.

The trek to the hotel was slow and painful. The boys were bruised and their muscles ached.

"A fine lot of fighters we look like," said Burt, managing a grin.

"Just the same," Dave spoke up, "I'll bet Nancy, Bess, and George will be glad to see us."

The policeman asked, "By any chance are you speaking of Miss Nancy Drew?"

The boys' surprise was evident. "You know her?" Ned asked unbelievingly.

The officer grinned. "Miss Drew is the one who telephoned headquarters. She was fearful you would be attacked."

"And she was right!" Ned said ruefully.

When the four reached the hotel, Nancy, Bess,

and George were waiting for them. The girls were aghast at their friends' disheveled condition, and amazed when they heard that Swahili Joe and another man had joined Brown and Ross.

"It must have been prearranged," Nancy said. "Oh, how can I ever thank you for risking your lives?"

"As fighters I don't think we rate very high," Burt spoke up. "I'll bet those men, Brown and Ross, are ex-prize fighters!"

The boys went upstairs immediately to get a long sleep before taking off for Mombasa in the morning. The girls went to their room, but talked a long time about the new turn in the mystery. George was particularly interested in the fact that Swahili Joe was in Nairobi when Ross had indicated that he was in Mombasa.

"He and the other man with him must have planned to meet Brown and Ross on that street. They were to be told what the Indians had found out from you, Nancy, about the spider sapphire."

Bess was sure they had more dire motives than that. "I hope the police catch them."

Before Nancy left her room the next morning, she telephoned police headquarters to find out if the four assailants had been captured. To her disappointment the men were still at large.

Bess was worried. "This means that strong-man Joe can keep on harming us," she said.

"We'll just have to keep our eyes open," George

retorted. She grinned. "He won't dare try another baboon trick on me!"

Nancy and her friends met in the lobby. The three boys looked refreshed but carried a few battle scars. Ned had a slightly blackened eye, Burt's forehead wore a lump, and Dave had a bandage on his left hand.

"Our heroes!" George teased.

The ride to the airfield and in the plane to Mombasa proved to be uneventful. There was no sign of their enemies. The young people hoped that for a time at least they had left their troubles behind.

When the plane landed, the Emerson group went at once to claim their baggage. Due to the large number of passengers, there were a great many suitcases rolling along the conveyor belt.

Finally Nancy spotted the large suitcase initialed ND. As her fingers reached for it, she noticed that a paper had been tied around the handle with a cord.

It occurred to Nancy that this might be a warning note! She grabbed the bag off the conveyor belt, set it on the floor, and immediately untied the paper. To her surprise there was nothing on either side of it.

She held the paper up to the light to look for any hidden writing. Apparently there was no message on the paper, so she tossed it into the nearby trash basket.

By this time Ned's bag had come along and he removed it from the conveyor belt with his left hand and grabbed Nancy's in his right.

They went outside and found a large taxi to accommodate three couples. It had a big luggage compartment in the rear. Their bags, as well as those of Bess, George, Burt, and Dave, were put into it, then the six Emersonians started for the hotel.

They had not gone more than a mile when Nancy's hands began to burn and itch. She scratched them instinctively, but this made them smart furiously.

"My hands are all red and they burn," she told the others.

"Mine too," said Ned as he held them up.

Suddenly a thought came to Nancy. "Somebody must have put acid on the handle of my suitcase! It's eating into our hands!"

CHAPTER XVII

Telltale Film

In another minute the pain in Nancy's and Ned's hands became unbearable. She leaned forward and spoke to the taxi driver, requesting him to stop at a drugstore. He put on speed and soon parked in front of Albert's Pharmacy.

Nancy and Ned jumped out of the taxi and ran inside. A short, energetic Englishman, seeing them rush in, hurried up behind the counter.

"I'm Mr. Albert," he said. "Is something wrong?"

"Yes. We got acid on our hands by accident," Ned told him.

"Please," Nancy spoke up, "may we have some oil quick to put on our hands?"

Mr. Albert looked at the reddened hands.

"Are you sure it is oil that you want?"

The couple's hands hurt so badly they could

hardly stand still. Fidgeting about, Nancy pleaded with the proprietor. "We don't know what the acid is, so I figure oil is the best thing."

"Well, perhaps you're right," Mr. Albert conceded. "Once when I was a boy—"

Nancy lost patience. "Please, please bring us any kind of oil at once!"

The man blinked, then reached up to a shelf behind him and brought down a bottle of mineral oil. He opened it for them and the suffering couple poured it liberally on their hands.

By this time Mr. Albert looked a little worried. "I will give you the name of a good doctor," he said. "Nobody should ignore a dreadful condition like that. Where have you been?"

Nancy and Ned hardly heard the loquacious man. Though the pain in their hands had eased a bit, both felt that if they could only douse them into oil up to the wrists, there would be a better chance of it penetrating the skin and offsetting the effects of the acid.

"Mr. Albert," said Nancy "would you please bring us basins so that we can put our whole hands into oil?"

The druggist seemed loath to do this. He acted afraid to have them in his shop.

"Listen, Mr. Albert," Ned said, "I know we are a lot of trouble to you but this is an emergency. No telling what might happen to us before we could get to a doctor."

The man gazed at Ned for several seconds, as if reluctant to accede to his request. Finally he invited them into a back room and brought down two small basins from a shelf. He poured large quantities of mineral oil into each. Nancy and Ned submerged their hands.

Mr. Albert continued to make pessimistic statements. "That acid could be poisonous and already be going through your system," he said dolefully.

"I'm sure it hasn't," Nancy said. She took her hands out of the oil. "All the burning has stopped."

Ned tested his. "Mine seem to be all right."

By this time Bess and George had come to see what was happening. They were relieved to hear that Nancy and Ned were better and ready to go.

Ned paid the druggist for the mineral oil and Nancy thanked him for his kindness. Once more the group set off.

The main part of Mombasa was situated on a large island and was reached by crossing a causeway. There was a large harbor with ocean liners and cargo vessels from many countries tied up.

The taxi went directly to an ocean-front hotel, with beautiful gardens and a swimming pool.

"Isn't this attractive?" Bess exclaimed.

Professor and Mrs. Stanley and the rest of the group were waiting for them on the steps of the portico. Nancy and Ned did not mention what had happened.

Burt insisted upon staying behind to take care of the baggage. He wrapped a newspaper around the handle of Nancy's bag before picking it up and refused to let either the taxi driver or porter touch it. Burt carried the suitcase to his own room and scrubbed the handle thoroughly with soap and water before delivering it to Nancy's room.

As he came in with the bag, Burt said, "Nancy, who do you think put the acid on the handle?"

"I can't name any one person," she answered, "but I'm sure it was one of the people connected with the spider sapphire mystery."

George spoke up. "It must have been done in Nairobi. Let's hope the villains have been left behind!"

Nancy was sure they had not been, but she did not intend to let this latest vicious act of her enemies deter her from continuing her detective work.

The Stanleys had arranged that the Emerson safari be given an early lunch so they could have a full afternoon for sightseeing. The incident of the suitcase had not been told to anyone but the Stanleys, who were solicitous and worried. Nancy and Ned assured them their hands felt all right.

"I have arranged separate tours for you young folks," said the professor.

He explained that several taxis had been hired. Nancy, Bess, George, and Gwen would go in one.

Aunt Millie Stanley smiled. "The professor and

I thought that the girls might be interested in different things from the boys. Your drivers have been instructed where to take you."

In a short time the taxis arrived. The four girls climbed into the first one and the driver set off. He was a pleasant, smiling black, who spoke Swahili and perfect English.

"First I thought you would be interested in seeing our many fruit markets," he said. "You know Africa is noted for its melons, pineapples, and berries."

He drove to a wide thoroughfare with fruit stalls on both sides of the street.

"Look!" Bess exclaimed. "I've never seen such big oranges in my life!"

Presently Nancy asked the driver if it would be permissible for her to take a couple of snapshots of a street scene. She knew that African blacks often did not like to have their pictures taken.

"I think it will be all right."

Nancy stepped out of the car and took one picture lengthwise of the street and one of a fruit stand. As she got back into the taxi, a tall, muscular black came racing across the street. He began waving a fist at her and speaking rapidly in Swahili.

"What is he saying?" she asked the driver.

"He is demanding your camera, because you took his picture."

*"Give me film or I have you arrested!" the man
said in halting English*

"But I didn't," Nancy replied. "I snapped the whole fruit stand from way over here."

The tall man continued to gesticulate and talk rapidly. By this time a crowd had gathered around the car.

"Why does he want the camera?" George asked.

The driver explained that people who belong to certain tribes believe that if their picture is snapped it will take away their soul.

"I see," said Nancy. "But I didn't snap this person's picture."

The tall man shook his fist at her again and said in halting English, "You give me film or I have you arrested!"

"Don't you do it, Nancy!" George cried out, but Bess and Gwen were terrified and begged her to turn the film over to him.

At that moment they all noticed a tall, handsome black officer hurrying toward them. He wore a white suit and helmet.

Smiling, he listened to the protestor's demand, then said to Nancy, "Please tell me your side of the story."

She explained. Apparently he believed her, for he turned to the tall man, spoke a few sentences in Swahili, and dismissed him with a wave of his hand.

The fruit dealer was reluctant to give in, but was finally persuaded to go back to his stand. The policeman scattered the crowd and the taxi drove off.

"Oh my!" said Bess. "I was scared silly. I think I'm going to faint!"

George turned to her cousin with a withering look. "Don't be a ninny," she said.

As they drove through one street after another, the girls were intrigued by the costumes of the Indian and the Arab citizens. Some men were wearing turbans with feathers stuck in them, others red fezzes. Nearly everyone wore sandals, but many of the blacks were barefoot.

Their guide stopped near a Hindu temple. It was a beautiful white, gold-domed building. A long courtyard led to a high-roofed portico with several steps leading up to it. A sign reminded the visitors to remove their shoes.

"Oh, look ahead!" Bess whispered.

As the four girls walked through the portico, they stopped to admire a large oblong pedestal on which rested the image of a white cow. It was gaily decorated with garlands of flowers and scarfs. Gwen asked the meaning of this.

"I've read," Nancy told her, "that in the Hindu religion the cow is a sacred animal and is never killed or eaten."

At the end of the portico and down several steps was a small room. Here were priests and worshipers, bowls of what looked like grain, and pots of incense. Since the visitors did not understand the significance, they bowed politely to those inside and turned away.

The next stop was in a commercial area where ivory auctions took place twice a year. Buyers came from all over the world. The warehouse manager showed the girls around. Tusks of elephant and rhino ivory lay on the floor.

"Is this made into jewelry and figurines?" Bess asked him.

"No, Kenya ivory is too soft. Most of it is used for billiard balls. Hard ivory comes from Uganda. It goes to Hong Kong and Japan for carving."

Nancy stepped among the great tusks. Near the end of the building were two huge elephant's feet. Nancy felt them and was surprised that they were covered with long bristly hairs.

When she returned to the entrance, George was just saying, "What would a rhino tusk be worth?"

"In an auction the price varies," the manager replied. "But the last one I sold brought seven hundred dollars."

"Whee!" George exclaimed. "When I saw those mean rhinos at Treetops Inn, I had no idea they were worth so much money!"

Bess giggled. "You'd have to pay me a lot more than seven hundred dollars to capture one."

The girls thanked the warehouse manager and

returned to the taxi. Their driver took a side road which led to a village of wood carvers.

The natives lived in attractive wooden houses. Beyond them was an open-air, thatched-roof "factory" where carved figures of animals and ceremonial masks were made from mahogany tree trunks.

Groups of men were chipping out the rough statuettes, others were doing the more delicate carving. Some workers were sandpapering and still others doing the final polishing. The results were satin-smooth, graceful figures of wild animals and every type of mask from pleasant-looking to the most grotesque.

Nancy went up to one of the series of small shops where the objects were displayed on rugs on the ground. "My father would love this," she said to the other girls, picking out a rhino. She also bought a duiker for her Aunt Eloise and an eland for Hannah Gruen.

Nancy paid for the articles. As the shopkeeper gave her change, he suddenly stared at Nancy and said, "You follow me!"

Nancy was startled. She had thought these people friendly. What was going to happen now?

The man, as if sensing her surprise, added, "All girls come! I make you death mask!"

CHAPTER XVIII

A Trick of Memory

"A death mask!" Bess shrieked. "Nancy, this is another threat! Let's get away from here as fast as we can!"

It was the shopkeeper's turn to look startled. "You are afraid of something?" he asked. "I mean no harm. I want to give gift to this nice young lady. She has lovely face. I have special artist to make likeness."

"But you said death mask," Bess told him.

The man shrugged. "Our people make them so relatives can enjoy the face after people are dead. Maybe your papa would like to have this if something happen to you? No harm come to you in this village."

Reassured, Nancy and the other girls followed the man to a tree-shaded area where a lone wood carver sat cross-legged on the ground working. He was an old man with an ingenuous smile.

He requested Nancy to seat herself on the ground, to raise her chin and hold very still. The other girls watched in fascination as the man's light fingers carefully chipped at a block of wood. In a short time the likeness to Nancy's features could be seen plainly. Soon he indicated he no longer needed her as a model and she was free to roam about until the mask was finished.

"He's very talented," Gwen remarked.

The others thought so too. Now they wandered about the village. The children were very good-looking and grinned most of the time. Nancy inquired if it was all right to take pictures and was told Yes. Once she started, the children crowded around, each one wanting to be in every picture. In a short time Nancy's film was used up.

The girls walked through the various areas, watching the deft fingers that produced the beautiful handiwork. Several times Nancy asked the workers if they knew a guide named Tizam. Each one shook his head.

Finally the old artist beckoned to them and they hurried over. He said the mask would be ready soon—a worker was giving the piece its final polish.

When Nancy queried him about Tizam, the wood carver's eyes lit up. "I know Tizam. He is very fine wood carver."

"Really?" Nancy was surprised that no one had told her this before. Perhaps he was not the same

Tizam whom she was trying to find. "Was he also a guide?"

"Yes. Last time I hear of him he take party out from Nairobi."

"What became of him?" Nancy inquired.

The old man said he did not know. He had not seen or heard of Tizam in a long time.

Nancy was excited by the idea that if Tizam were a wood carver this might be a real clue to his whereabouts. She asked the old man whether Tizam specialized in any type of figures.

"Yes. He always make statue of three gazelles together."

"That's unusual," George spoke up. She thought she knew what was racing through Nancy's mind.

"You're going to start hunting for some of Tizam's work?"

As Nancy nodded, a boy brought her finished mask to the old man. He smiled.

"You like this? You are satisfied?"

"Indeed I am," Nancy replied. "Of course one never knows what one looks like. What do you girls think?"

"It's an amazing likeness," Bess told her.

The elderly wood carver examined his work inside and out very carefully before summoning Nancy to his side. "I want to show you special secret thing I put in."

He turned the mask over and pointed to the

eye sockets. They had been covered with tiny wooden doors. Now the wood carver lifted up each one with a fingernail. A tiny spring with a miniature wooden peg held the doors in place. The sockets were empty.

"This good hiding place," he said. "You keep money or jewelry in here. Nobody think to look and steal."

Nancy congratulated him on his ingenuity, and expressed her appreciation for the extra effort he had put into making the marvelous mask. Nancy took it from him and asked how much she owed.

A hurt look came over the artist's face. "I take no money for this. It is gift for you. Enjoy it. Maybe you give it to your papa and tell him I once had daughter like you. She older now. Have eight children." He pointed toward some whose pictures Nancy had taken.

"You are very fortunate and very kind," Nancy said. "Since you will not let me pay you for the mask, at least I can send you copies of the pictures I took of your grandchildren."

He smiled. "That very nice reward."

The girls said good-by and walked back toward their taxi. When they passed the shop where Nancy had made the purchases, she showed the mask to the owner. The man grinned broadly.

"I am glad the old man did such good work," he said "Did he put in the secret eye sockets?"

Nancy showed him and he said this custom was

still followed by some African blacks. A mask was put over the face of the deceased person and precious belongings inserted into the sockets.

When the girls reached their taxi, Nancy held up the mask for their guide to see, then slipped it into her large shopping bag. As they continued their tour of the city, she asked him to take them to various shops where wood carvings were sold. The driver looked a little puzzled, having just taken them to the best one. But he merely nodded.

They returned to the heart of the city and stopped at one shop where a variety of gift items were sold. The girls thoroughly combed the shelves and counters but saw no carved pieces of three gazelles together. The searchers went into several other shops.

Finally in one George exclaimed, "Nancy, here are three gazelles!"

The girl detective ran over to look. At almost the same time Bess and Gwen discovered two others. They were exquisite pieces, but there was no artist's name carved into the bottom.

Nancy approached a clerk and asked if she might see the store owner. She was taken to a little office at the rear of the shop. The owner was a very pleasant English woman.

"I am very much interested in these pieces of three gazelles," Nancy said. "Would you mind telling me who the artist is?"

The woman said, "I do not remember but I will look it up."

She took a ledger from a shelf and began to turn the pages. After checking her list of purchases, she pointed to one entry. "The man's name is Huay. He is a black and like so many of those people is a very fine wood carver."

"I will buy this," Nancy said, indicating the one in her hand. "Does Mr. Huay have a shop near here?"

"Right around the corner. There are some old stone buildings. You'll see an alleyway with a gate. It's the only one on the block. Mr. Huay's shop is at the rear."

Nancy paid for the figurine and the girls hurried outside. They told their driver they were going to a shop around the corner and would return soon.

The girls found the gated alleyway easily, let themselves in, and walked to the rear. A fine-looking black sat cross-legged on the floor near the doorway of his shop. He was carving gazelles. At the girls' approach, he looked up.

"Mr. Huay?" Nancy asked.

The man arose and laid down his work. "Yes, miss. May I help you?"

Nancy was trying not to stare at the man, but instinct told her she had found Tizam, using an assumed name. He looked very much like Madame Bulawaya!

Many thoughts raced through her mind. Was he hiding because of something he had done? If not, then he must be suffering from amnesia. Could she startle him into a confession or recollection?

"I have just purchased one of your beautiful pieces, Mr. Tizam," she said.

The wood carver looked at her blankly. "Yes, that is one of my pieces, but my name is Huay."

The other girls looked at Nancy, wondering how she would proceed. They too were convinced that this man was indeed Tizam and that he had lost his memory.

"Have you been here long?" Nancy asked him.

"I am not sure," the wood carver replied, and a frown crossed his forehead.

"As you have probably guessed, we girls are from the United States. Just before we flew to Africa, we attended a concert by Madame Lilia Bulawaya."

Nancy paused and carefully watched the effect on the man.

"Oh yes, Lilia," Huay said. Then again his eyes clouded. There was no mistaking the fact, however, that there had been a slight semblance of recognition in the name.

Nancy now tried a new tack. Softly she began to hum the Swahili lullaby which Madame Bulawaya had taught her. In a moment Mr. Huay began to hum with her.

Bess thought excitedly, "I just know something is going to happen!"

When Nancy finished the tune, she began to sing it again, this time with the words. Mr. Huay smiled and joined her. The light in his eyes became clearer and clearer.

When the song ended, he said, "Where did you learn those Swahili words?"

"From your sister, Madame Lilia Bulawaya."

"Yes, yes of course," the man said.

Bess could not refrain from asking, "You remember her, don't you, Mr. Huay?"

The wood carver turned puzzled eyes on the girl. "You called me Mr. Huay? That is not my name. It is Tizam."

The girls could have jumped for joy. They had found the guide, long supposed dead but only suffering from amnesia!

As memory fluttered back to Tizam, he was besieged with questions. But he remembered nothing from the time a lioness began to maul him and he had blacked out.

"Perhaps you girls can tell me more about my recent life than I can," he said.

Nancy told what little she knew, including the fact that a guide named Butubu had saved Tizam's life by killing the lioness before he had a chance to maul Tizam to death.

"I shall go to Nairobi someday and find this Butubu to thank him," the wood carver said. "I am curious to know how I got to Mombasa and rented this shop. Perhaps I can find out from my neighbors. But the most important thing now is to get in touch with my sister. Do you know where she is?"

Nancy said she did not know exactly, but thought her friend Ned Nickerson could find out through the college where Madame Bulawaya had given a concert.

"I'll ask Ned to cable as soon as we get back to out hotel," she promised. "Mr. Tizam," Nancy added, "when we visited the tribe that befriended you, they told us that a couple of times you had made a certain remark. It was 'I must go to Mombasa at once and report those thieves to the police.' What did you mean?"

Tizam looked puzzled. To jog his memory, Nancy asked, "Could it have had anything to do with the famous spider sapphire?"

The wood carver stood up very straight and his eyes blazed.

CHAPTER XIX

The Dungeon Trap

FOR a few moments Nancy began to wonder if she had undone all the good she had accomplished in restoring Tizam's memory. His eyes continued to stare into space and smolder with anger. The girls glanced at one another and waited in fear for him to speak.

With a deep breath Tizam finally said, "It all comes back to me now. Just before I was attacked by the lioness I was watching, I heard two men speaking in English. They were evidently spying on me, but thought I did not understand the language.

"I could not see either man and did not hear them call each other by name," Tizam went on, "but I judged they were from India, because every once in a while they would slip in an Indian word."

"Were they talking about you?" Nancy queried.

"Yes. They said they were going to take a valuable spider sapphire in Mombasa and then start a rumor blaming the theft on me!"

"And they did just that," George spoke up, recalling Mr. Tagore's accusation.

Although Tizam was still angry over this injustice, he spoke softly to the girls.

"I was sure those two men intended to kill me, so I could never report them. I turned to confront them, forgetting the lioness. At that moment the animal attacked. The two men apparently thought I had been killed and in order to save their own lives I guess they ran away."

George told Tizam that the guide Butubu who had saved his life had spotted a lioness, evidently the companion of the one he had killed. It sprang at him so he too had run.

"By the time he got back to help you, Mr. Tizam, you had disappeared."

When Nancy revealed that the spider sapphire was gone, and told how she had become involved in the mystery, the wood carver looked amazed.

"Did those men say where they intended to take the gem after they had stolen it?" Nancy asked.

Tizam thought a moment. "They mentioned something about a dungeon and Vasco da Gama. He was a Portuguese explorer who came here many years ago. A street was named after him."

"Then it's probably in an old part of town," Nancy surmised.

"It is," Tizam replied.

Nancy said she would investigate the dungeon as soon as possible. In the meantime her friend Ned Nickerson would cable the college to try to find out Madame Lilia Bulawaya's address.

"Are you sure you will be all right here alone?" Bess asked the wood carver.

He smiled. "I think so. But perhaps, until the mystery is solved, I had better remain as Mr. Huay." The others agreed this was a wise decision.

When the girls returned to the hotel, stories of the day's events were exchanged with Ned, Burt, and Dave, but none could compete with the astounding adventure of finding Tizam.

"I'll cable the college at once," Ned offered, and went to do this.

The others sat in a quiet corner of the lobby, discussing how to go about locating the spider sapphire. "I think we should alert the police," Bess said positively.

George did not agree. "Wouldn't it be more sensible to go to Mr. Tagore? He seemed honest to me, and after all the spider sapphire belongs to him."

Nancy, who had been deep in thought, spoke up. "I now suspect not only Jahan and Dhan, but Mr. Tagore's secretary Rhim Rao. I suggest that we go right to that dungeon."

Gwen, in the meantime, had asked to be excused and had gone to her room. Nancy asked the desk clerk where Vasco da Gama Street was and was directed to a section some distance from the hotel.

"You had better take a taxi," he said.

Nancy went back to her friends and there was more discussion on how to proceed. Finally it was decided that Bess and Dave would pay a friendly call on Mr. Tagore. The couple would not mention what they had learned or what their group suspected. The main reason for their visit would be to check on the secretary, Rhim Rao.

The other four would go directly to Vasco da Gama Street. If they could find the dungeon, George and Burt would stay outside and act as lookouts. Nancy and Ned would enter and search for the missing spider sapphire.

One taxi carried Bess and Dave to Mr. Tagore's home. Another took the others to the old part of the city where Vasco da Gama Street was located. They got out and dismissed the driver. Smiling, Nancy approached a small, barefoot boy. She asked him if he knew where there was a dungeon on this street.

The grinning little native said, "Americans ask me funny questions. Yes, I know where a dungeon is. I show you."

Ned handed the boy a coin and the four followed him down the street. On either side were ancient stone buildings. The boy stopped in front of one.

"No one inside," he said. "You go to dungeon alone. Many sightseers do. I will not enter. Evil spirits might be in there."

He scampered off. George and Burt took up posts on opposite sides of the street. George walked across while Burt remained near an unlocked basement door. Nancy and Ned knocked. Receiving no answer, they stepped inside.

The place was dank and dark and at once the searchers turned on their flashlights. A steep incline led them to a door which opened into a wine cellar with a great many kegs. It was apparent that the place had not been used in some time.

"I'm sure nobody would hide a precious gem in one of these kegs of wine," Nancy remarked. "It might mar the luster."

Nevertheless, Ned shook each keg to be sure of this. He and Nancy heard nothing but the sloshing of wine.

Next, they began an examination of the walls, which had once been covered with plaster, but now most of it had crumbled away, revealing the rock foundation. There was no noticeable hiding place in the wall Ned was examining.

Nancy had turned her attention to another wall where the upper section set back about six inches making a narrow earthen shelf. As she beamed her light along it, Nancy saw that in one spot the dirt and plaster had been dug out, then replaced. She called softly to Ned.

He held both flashlights as Nancy quickly removed the soft dirt with her fingers. At the bottom of the hole lay a gold box. The two young detectives held their breath. Had they solved the mystery?

Hoping against hope, Nancy opened the box. Inside lay a gleaming sapphire and in its center rested a spider!

"This is it!" she whispered excitedly, and asked Ned to hold the light closer. "The gem's not synthetic! See, that spider has no spinnerets!"

The couple continued to stare at the magnificent gem, which sparkled like a weird, unearthly fire.

Finally Ned said, "Nancy, you've done it again! You've solved a very puzzling mystery!"

She smiled at him, then said, "I think we had better get out of here as soon as possible and take this to Mr. Tagore."

"You're right."

Still carrying the box, Nancy led the way to the door. It would not open.

Ned yanked and pulled at the latch but it did not budge. "Someone has locked us in!" he said.

Nancy's heart sank. Any minute their enemies might come in and take the spider sapphire away from her!

"I must hide it," she thought. "But where?" There was no likely place in the dungeon.

Just then she thought of the mask which was in her shopping bag. Handing it to Ned, she whispered, "Help me!"

She handed him the jewel box, then reached into the bag and pulled out the mask. Quickly she lifted the little door behind one of the eye sockets and slipped the precious gem inside it. Then she tucked the mask back into her bag.

At the same instant she and Ned heard a sliding door scraping open. They looked toward the sound which came from the opposite side of the room. A concealed door was slowly being opened. Two men in Indian dress walked in.

Jahan and Dhan!

The latter was carrying a whip which he began to brandish.

"So you thought you would spoil our little game!" Jahan said. "You underrated us."

He reached toward Ned's hand and grabbed the jewel box. Nancy had a fleeting hope that he would not open it, that the men would leave, and she and Ned escape.

But her hope was shattered when Dhan ordered excitedly, "Open that box!"

Jahan did so. He gave a cry of dismay upon finding it empty. He screamed at Nancy and Ned, "Where's the spider sapphire?"

The couple made no response. The two Indians

were furious. As Dhan snapped and cracked the whip, it came within inches of the couple.

"Search them!" he cried.

Jahan carefully went through Ned's pockets, then he turned to Nancy's shopping bag. Her heart almost stopped beating. Would he discover the hiding place of the spider sapphire?

She and Ned gave no sign by the expression on their faces that they were worried. Though Jahan searched carefully, he hardly looked at the mask and did not even turn it over.

"The jewel's not here," he reported to his father.

The older man, his face livid with rage, cracked the whip several times. Finally he faced Nancy.

There was a cruel, unrelenting look in his eyes as he said to her, "Tell us where the spider sapphire is or I'll use this whip on your friend here!"

CHAPTER XX

A Double Cross Backfires

ALMOST speechless with terror and yet deter-
mined not to give up the spider sapphire, Nancy
jumped in front of Ned.

"Don't you dare strike him!" she cried out.

Jahan and Dhan were taken aback by the young
detective's defiance. As Ned stepped in front of
her so she would not be harmed, Nancy began to
talk fast.

"No matter what you do to us," she said, "it
will not keep you from being arrested. Your whole
scheme has been found out!"

Dhan stopped the whip in mid-air. As he was
trying to make up his mind whether to strike Ned,
the squeaky sliding door opened a bit farther.
Swahili Joe walked into the room.

He spoke to the men in Swahili, then advanced
toward the prisoners.

"Stand back, Nancy!" Ned ordered. "I'm not

going to let this big baboon pull another kidnapping!"

Nancy went on, "There's a police net around here. All three of you will be caught."

"They can't arrest us," said Dhan, "because we have not done anything."

"Oh no?" said Ned. "You nearly smothered Nancy with a plastic-lined sack and stuck a warning note in her hand. And you burned all the clothes and suitcases of Miss Drew and two other girls. You even stole their jewelry. After you kidnapped me, you sabotaged Miss Drew's car and tried to keep her from flying to Africa by phoning her father's office that I wasn't coming. And you put acid on the handle of her suitcase to delay her work. It might have scarred her for life!" The men did not deny the accusations.

Nancy's eyes snapped. "You men stole the spider sapphire from Mr. Tagore," she said. "Then you came to the United States and tried several ways to get the synthetic gem in the River Heights museum to bring back here and put in place of the original—even hoped to blackmail Mr. Ramsey with a sign saying his gem was a stolen one."

"It was not our idea," Jahan spoke up.

"We suspected that," Nancy continued. "It was Mr. Tagore's secretary, Rhim Rao, who engineered the whole scheme. He paid for your trip to our country. You came there under the false name of Prasad."

The two Indians stared in amazement. Swahili Joe stood looking blankly at Nancy. Apparently he did not know what she was talking about.

Ned took up the story. "You used Swahili Joe as your strong-arm man. The poor fellow is under your domination. After his bad fall in the circus, he became an easy dupe for you people. I don't know what the penalty is in your country for kidnapping, but he has a count against him up at Treetops for carrying off one of our girls."

The three men stared speechless at Nancy and Ned. They translated a bit of the conversation to Swahili Joe, who suddenly looked frightened. Nancy went on with her accusations, to gain time until she and Ned could be rescued. She mentioned that Ross and Brown were part of the gang and the Indians did not deny this.

"Tizam—whom you planned to kill and who you thought was killed by a lion—is alive," Nancy said. At that, Jahan and Dhan actually jumped in astonishment.

She asked suddenly, "Do you trust Rhim Rao?"

The two Indians exchanged glances, then Jahan finally admitted that Rao had thought up the whole scheme. "He was going to collect the insurance for Mr. Tagore and later sell the spider sapphire. But the company has been making a thorough investigation, and he became a little worried. When he heard about the synthetic gem in the United States, he thought if he could hand it to his employer as the real sapphire, he would be safe and Mr. Tagore would not know the difference."

Nancy thought, "So Rhim Rao doesn't know about the spinnerets! Mr. Tagore would have detected the substitution at once!"

Dhan now seemed ready to talk. "Rhim Rao never told us where he hid the spider sapphire. He promised us our share when he sold it."

Ned spoke up. "He couldn't have sold it. The gem would have been traced too easily."

"He was going to break it up into smaller stones," Jahan explained.

Dhan said, "We have been following you people. When you came into this building, we thought you had found the hiding place of the spider sapphire. Both of us know this old building well. We locked the outside door to this dungeon and then went around to the inside and came down here."

His son's face took on an angry expression. "Since you two didn't find the spider sapphire, I guess Rao hid it somewhere else. Maybe he has already sold it and is going to freeze out my father and me."

Nancy and Ned did not comment, but it

served their purpose to let the men think this. Now maybe they would release their prisoners.

Dhan spoke up again. "Rhim Rao is a thief. He steals from Mr. Tagore, his employer, all the time. This is how he got the money to send us to River Heights. Mr. Tagore doesn't suspect his secretary. In fact, it was Rhim Rao who told him Tizam had taken the spider sapphire."

Suddenly Dhan said, "We have talked too much. If we let this girl and her friend go, they'll tell the police. Let's leave them locked in and get out of here!"

The two Indians and Swahili Joe were about to depart through the sliding door when there was a commotion outside. Several police entered the dungeon. They quickly arrested the three Africans and explained that when George and Burt had seen them enter the building, George had notified the authorities.

As Nancy and the others reached the street, George and Burt rushed up, relieved to see that she and Ned had not been harmed.

"When I saw that whip, I wanted to go right in after those men," said George, "but Burt wouldn't let me." She smiled. "And I wouldn't let him go either. We might all have been trapped and unable to summon the police."

"You did the right thing," one of the officers told her. "Do I understand other people are involved in this theft of the spider sapphire?"

Nancy quickly told what she knew and said that two friends of hers had gone to the Tagore home to keep an eye on Rhim Rao.

"I think we should go there," she said, "and give Mr. Tagore his spider sapphire."

"And arrest Rhim Rao," Ned added.

At that announcement Jahan's and Dhan's eyes bulged. "You found it?" Jahan screamed. "Rhim Rao didn't double-cross us after all?"

Nancy did not reply. Instead, she told the police where she had found it and they agreed she should be the one to return it. Two detectives would go to the Tagore home with her and arrest Rhim Rao if he were there.

"In order to avoid suspicion," said one of the detectives, "I think you four young people had better go in one cab. We will follow in another. If Rhim Rao suspects the police are after him, he will certainly try to get away."

Taxis were summoned. When Nancy and her friends reached the Tagore home, they saw Bess and Dave just coming out. They were followed by an Indian about forty-five years old.

Ned paid the taxi driver and the visitors walked forward. "Hello!" Bess called cheerfully. The others knew she was eager to ask them how they had made out, but her expression gave no sign of this. "I would like you to meet Mr. Rhim Rao," she said, and presented him to her four friends.

Nancy kept up a running conversation until she

saw the detectives' taxi coming. As soon as the policemen got out, she introduced them. Rhim Rao looked puzzled, but the expression on his face changed when the detectives announced that he was under arrest.

"This is preposterous!" Rao shouted.

His further protests were interrupted by the appearance of Mr. Tagore. He bowed to the callers, then asked what the trouble was.

"These men are trying to arrest me and I have done nothing!" Rhim Rao exclaimed.

During the conversation, Nancy had taken the mask from her shopping bag. Now she turned it over and lifted the tiny door back of one eye.

"Here is your missing spider sapphire, Mr. Tagore," she announced, and handed it over. The owner stared unbelievingly. "You found it? Where?"

"Perhaps you should ask Mr. Rhim Rao where he hid it," she answered.

The thief became bold in his reply. "Me!" he cried out. "I know nothing about the disappearance of this gem. I am delighted that it has been recovered."

Ned gave him a dark look. "Your friends Jahan and Dhan have confessed," he said. "They are in jail."

Hearing this, Rhim Rao lost all his bravado. He changed into a sniveling, pleading individual, assuring his employer that no harm had been intended. Mr. Tagore stared at him in disgust. "Your defense can be brought up in court. Take him away, men."

When the excitement had died down, Mr. Tagore invited his callers to enter the house. He led them through a richly carpeted hall to a rear garden. It was filled with beautiful flowers, and had a large pool partly filled with water lilies. At the end of it stood an attractive white summerhouse.

"Let us go over there and talk," their host suggested.

"Isn't this picturesque?" Bess whispered as they followed Mr. Tagore.

A servant, wearing a white tight-fitting suit and a bright-red turban, entered the summerhouse, carrying a huge tray. Tea was served and with it delicious pastries and a bowl of fruit. As they ate, Mr. Tagore asked for full details of the young people's adventures since meeting them at the Mount Kenya Safari Club.

At the end he said, "I must talk with Tizam. You say he is not far away. Perhaps I could send for him."

Ned offered to go for the wood carver. While he was gone, the others continued to exchange stories about the mystery. Nancy asked Mr. Tagore if he had ever heard of men named Ross, Brown, Ramon, and Sharma.

"I do not know the first two, but they are probably part of Rhim Rao's gang. I think we should ask our police to get in touch with the authorities in Nairobi and find out if the men have been picked up yet.

"Ramon and Sharma are friends of mine. They advised me some time ago not to put so much trust in Rhim Rao. Unfortunately I did not take their advice."

As Bess finished her second cup of tea, she said, "Mr. Tagore, do you know that at one point in solving this mystery we all distrusted you? Please forgive us."

George grinned. "We were even going to give back the necklaces you left for us."

Mr. Tagore chuckled. "I don't blame you one bit for mistrusting me. The disappearance of my gem was so strange it must have seemed to you like a fraud. Incidentally, sometime I should like to see the gem your friend Mr. Ramsey has produced. He must be an exceedingly fine chemist." Mr. Tagore went on to say that the jewelry he had given the girls was small reward for all they had done. When they refused anything more, he said, "It would give me pleasure to entertain your whole Emerson safari at a very special dinner Indian style."

"Thank you very much," said Nancy.

A few minutes later Ned arrived with Tizam, who had brought along several wood carvings of the three gazelles standing together. After introductions he presented the first figurine to Mr. Tagore, then handed one to each of the young people.

"I have had the pleasure," said the Indian, "of hearing your sister Madame Lilia Bulawaya sing. She has a remarkable voice."

Tizam smiled and said through the efforts of Mr. Nickerson she had been located and had already communicated with him. "I am very happy about this and will see her as soon as her tour in the United States is over."

Tizam turned to the young people. "The money she was raising through her concert tour to find me should go to Nancy Drew and her friends."

Again the Americans refused any remuneration for their work and Bess said, "We're just pleased to have had a part in solving the case."

This remark made Nancy realize her work was finished. But not for long. Soon she would be starting to solve the challenging mystery of *The Invisible Intruder*.

"Mr. Tizam," said Nancy, "wouldn't you like to see the spider sapphire?"

"Indeed I would," he replied.

When it was shown to him, he looked at it in astonishment. "It is an amazing gem."

"I should say," George spoke up, "that Nancy Drew has made this spider the most famous one that ever lived on this earth!"

Have you read the latest Dana Girls mystery by Carolyn Keene? It's called THE SECRET OF THE MINSTREL'S GUITAR and is one of another series by the author of the Nancy Drew Books. Louise and Jean Dana, like Nancy herself, meet and match the challenge of each new mystery. Here is a list of some of the thrilling adventures of the teen-age sister sleuths.

THE GHOST IN THE GALLERY
THE CLUE OF THE BLACK FLOWER
THE WINKING RUBY MYSTERY
THE SECRET OF THE SWISS CHALET
THE HAUNTED LAGOON
THE MYSTERY OF THE BAMBOO BIRD
THE SIERRA GOLD MYSTERY
THE SECRET OF LOST LAKE
THE MYSTERY OF THE STONE TIGER
THE RIDDLE OF THE FROZEN FOUNTAIN
THE SECRET OF THE SILVER DOLPHIN
MYSTERY OF THE WAX QUEEN

Publishers *Grosset & Dunlap* New York